You're invited

CREEPOVER ®

Don't Move a Muscle!

written by P. J. Night

SIMON SPOTLIGHT
New York   London   Toronto   Sydney   New Delhi

SIMON SPOTLIGHT
An imprint of Simon & Schuster Children's Publishing Division
1230 Avenue of the Americas, New York, New York 10020
First Simon Spotlight paperback edition July 2016
Copyright © 2016 by Simon & Schuster, Inc.
Minotaur and maze © 2016 by iStock/Thinkstock
All rights reserved, including the right of reproduction in whole or in part in any form.
SIMON SPOTLIGHT and colophon are registered trademarks of Simon & Schuster, Inc.
YOU'RE INVITED TO A CREEPOVER is a registered trademark of Simon & Schuster, Inc.
Text by Ann Hodgman
For information about special discounts for bulk purchases, please contact
Simon & Schuster Special Sales at 1-866-506-1949 or business@simonandschuster.com.
Designed by Nick Sciacca
Manufactured in the United States of America 0616 OFF
10 9 8 7 6 5 4 3 2 1
ISBN 978-1-4814-2922-1
ISBN 978-1-4814-2923-8 (eBook)
Library of Congress Catalog Card Number 2014935638

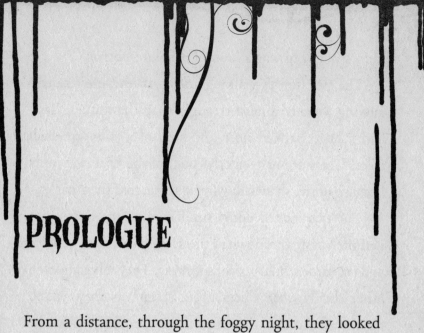

PROLOGUE

From a distance, through the foggy night, they looked like birds.

Hunched, huge birds, heads bent, moving slowly through a graveyard. No—not a graveyard—a garden full of stone sculptures.

The garden seemed like a peaceful spot. There were ornamental trees in antique clay pots, their branches occasionally brushing across the statues. Water bubbled gently from a small fountain. The statues—gods, goddesses, heroes, and soldiers from ancient Greek and Roman legends—stood alert and ready.

On closer inspection, though, some of the statues were . . . disturbing. Almost *too* realistic. Carved into each stone face was a look of absolute horror.

The two figures walking among them were strange-looking women, almost stranger than the statues. Each had a huge hooked nose and skin of a pale, greenish color. They seemed elderly, but maybe that was only because of the shawls drawn tightly across their backs.

The two looked oddly similar, not quite twins, but definitely sisters. They had the same harsh tone of voice and the same stilted way of speaking. They talked to each other shrilly, with traces of an accent, as they wound their way through the labyrinth of hedges toward the heart of the garden.

"Is this truly the right place for the new statue?" one said. The women had stopped walking now. They were standing in an empty patch of space on the garden's lawn.

"Yes." The other woman sounded impatient. "I have already told you. The ground is prepared."

"Still, I am not sure," insisted the first woman. "The new statue will be so lively. Perhaps a less visible spot would be better at first?"

"There is no time to change it now," answered her sister. "The new statue arrives soon. As you *also* already know. Besides, they are always lively at first."

"True, true," agreed the first woman. "I thought Anthony would never settle into his spot." She gave a small laugh. It was not a pleasant sound. "And Isabella here!" Mockingly she patted the arm of the statue next to her—a life-size woman holding a basket on her shoulder. "Tired of carrying so heavy a burden all this time, my dear?"

The statue stared motionless into the dark. But as a wavering shaft of moonlight broke through the fog, there was a flicker in the look of anguish on the statue's face.

"The constellations will be in alignment very soon," remarked the second woman as the sisters began pacing through the garden again. "It is an . . . unpredictable time. Strange things can happen."

But now someone else was coming. Footsteps could be heard treading the sidewalk toward the sisters. Through the fog, the figure of a boy became clearer and clearer. He looked to be fourteen or fifteen, with dark wavy hair and olive skin.

"I came to see if you wanted anything," he said.

"You know what we want," said the second woman with a half smile. "We want you to deliver that statue. On time."

The boy sighed. "It's not as easy as I'd expected."

"Easy or hard, we will have that statue," said the first woman. "The ground is prepared—"

"I know, I know," the boy interrupted.

The second woman snapped, "Do you not want your reward? We can always find someone else to do the job."

"No! I'll make it happen. I'll get you the statue."

"And then you will have the reward we promised," said the second woman. "Now we must all go in. There is much to do before daylight."

The two women pivoted in unison and began walking toward the exit. After a moment the boy followed, his steps dragging.

As the three vanished from sight, a cloud slid away from the moon.

Just then there was an odd rippling throughout the garden. Some of the statues seemed to shudder. Others looked as if they had shifted position ever so slightly—and then were suddenly frozen back in place. Was that the wind rustling the branches? Was somebody moving stealthily through the garden?

It couldn't be the statues, right?

Of course it couldn't.

CHAPTER 1

"And I want it to have a halter top. Or maybe spaghetti straps. Of *course* my mom says it can't be strapless."

"Mine won't let me get a black dress. She thinks it's too formal. But I found something online that I think she'll say is okay. It is so, so gorgeous."

"Well, my parents say they won't pay for a dress for an eighth-grade dance. But I've saved up a lot from babysitting."

Four girls were sitting at a lunch table in school. Three of them had been talking about clothes for ten minutes. Those ten minutes had seemed more like ten hours to Cora Nicolaides, the fourth girl at the table. The eighth-grade dance was in a couple of weeks. Her three best friends—Hailey, Amber, and Skye—had dates for it. Cora didn't.

Hailey must have sensed how Cora was feeling. "Sorry, Cor," she said. "This must all sound stupid."

"No, it's fine," Cora said honestly. "I'm interested. It's just . . . you know. I wish I could go too. The four of us have always done everything together."

"But you can go! Lots of people are going to the dance without a date!" objected Amber. "Just come on your own and hang out with us."

"Be bold," Skye added.

Easy for them to say, thought Cora. Her friends had enough self-confidence for thirty people. And why not? All three were smart, athletic, and pretty. Cora knew she was smart, but she hated sports. (Reading was what she liked.) Pretty? Hard to say. She liked her hair—a tumbling cloud of dark brown curls. Her green eyes and thick black lashes were okay too. But wasn't it really a person's expression that got other people's attention? And Cora was sure she looked too serious and shy for anyone to notice her.

Sometimes she wondered if Hailey, Amber, and Skye would have been her best friends if they hadn't all been in the same second-grade class. For so long they'd all been interested in similar things: crafts, animals, video games . . . but now the three other girls seemed to care much more about gossip. Who was going out with each other? Who was going to Brooke's party that weekend? Why had Aiden been grounded?

Cora was interested in those things too, of course, but only up to a point. Was that going to become a problem? What if the three other girls moved on—found a new friend who was more outgoing, more like them? Then Cora would be on her own. And a lot of the time she felt lonely enough already.

But now Cora realized she was starting to feel sorry for herself. *Don't wallow,* she thought. *It won't get you anywhere.*

"So when are you guys getting these dresses?" she asked cheerfully. "Because you *know* I have to approve them first."

"I was thinking this weekend would be good," said Amber. "Maybe we could all go together?"

"Yes!" said Cora. Quickly she checked the calendar on her phone. "Why don't we all go on Saturday afternoon? And then why don't you come over for a sleepover?"

Her friends all promised to check with their parents

as soon as they could. "Perfect. I can't wait to see what you guys pick out!" Cora said, hoping she sounded convincing.

Right then the bell rang to signal the end of lunch period. In the hustle to return trays and collect books, Cora felt free to drop the cheerful act. She sighed as she heaved her backpack onto her shoulder. The sleepover would be fun, she knew, but she also knew that most of their conversations would end up at the same place—the dance. Her friends would start by talking about the dresses they'd bought. Then the conversation would move on to their dates. And Cora would be nodding enthusiastically, trying to be a good sport.

Maybe I should buy a dress just in case, she thought. *I might suddenly get the courage to go. Or it's just possible that someone might—*

But she cut herself off midthought. She'd better face it. Unless she went to the dance alone, she wouldn't be going at all.

The middle school bus came so early in the morning, and took so long getting to school, that one of Cora's parents usually drove her and picked her up. Her dad was working from home today, so it would be his turn for pickup that afternoon. Cora took her time as she walked to the car-pool section of the parking lot after school. Her dad was usually a little late, and besides, she was deep in thought. It wasn't the dance that was on her mind this time—or at least not the actual dance. It was a problem from her math class. Her math teacher, Mr. Ferris, always made a big deal about how helpful math could be in real life. That afternoon he had come up with a problem that was obviously meant to be "timely."

The dance committee is setting up square tables for the eighth-grade dance. Each table seats four, and the committee may use as many tables as it needs. Tables may be pushed together, but no table arrangement may seat more than twelve. (Why? Because Mr. Ferris says so.) Show three different ways that sixteen couples could be seated for the dance.

Cora wished Mr. Ferris had written "thirty-two people" instead of "sixteen couples," but this was the kind of math question she liked. She was walking slowly along, staring at the ground and imagining different table arrangements, when someone suddenly crashed into her.

"Whoa! Sorry! I didn't see you."

Startled, Cora looked up at the boy who had just bumped into her. He was a little older than she—ninth or tenth grade, maybe?—and incredibly handsome. He had dark, wavy hair, an olive complexion, and eyes that were almost black. He was several inches taller than Cora, and he was smiling down at her. His smile was pretty incredible too.

"I—I'm the one who should be sorry," Cora stammered. "I was thinking about a math problem."

"And I was going too fast," said the boy. "Tell you what. We can both be sorry. How does that sound?"

Cora smiled shyly back at him. "Sounds good."

"I guess I just proved that haste really does make waste," said the boy. "Wait—that didn't come out right. It's never a waste to bump into a cute girl."

Cora could feel herself blushing.

"But," he continued, "I did drop all these postcards I'm supposed to be rushing to the post office."

Now Cora saw that a pile of cards was scattered all over the ground. "Let me help!" she said. "Seeing as I'm so sorry and all."

"Thanks—that'd be great. By the way, my name is Evan."

"I'm Cora. Do you go to school here?"

Evan was down on his knees scrambling for the postcards. He stopped for a second to gesture toward the high school across the parking lot and the football field beyond it. "Yup, right over there. I'm a freshman. I'm on my way to work."

"Work?"

Evan laughed. "Well, 'work' sounds better than 'after-school job,' don't you think?"

He was already on his feet and reaching out for the few postcards Cora had picked up. She handed them over reluctantly. If only there had been a lot more postcards so that Evan could have stayed longer! But it wasn't going to happen. He'd gotten all the cards back in order much too quickly.

"Gotta run—I'm already late," he said. "See you around." In a few seconds he had turned the corner and disappeared from sight.

Wistfully Cora watched him go. She had just had an actual conversation with a high school boy! Unfortunately, she would probably never see him again. . . .

"*Who* was *that*? He's *cute*." Hailey had come up from behind without Cora even noticing.

"He's definitely cute," Cora agreed. "His name is Evan. He's a freshman. He has a job after school. And that's probably all I'll ever know about him."

"I know one more thing. He dropped that card." When Hailey pointed, Cora realized that one of Evan's postcards was lying at her feet. She picked it up and looked at it more closely. The picture side had a black-and-white photo showing a cluster of statues on a lawn somewhere. Along the bottom were the words METAXAS SCULPTURE GARDEN PRESENTS . . .

"Presents what?" said Cora. She flipped the card over. "'The unveiling of our newest acquisition,'" she read aloud. "Oh—it's Sunday the eighteenth, the day after the dance."

"What's an acquisition?" asked Hailey.

"I think that's what museums call it when they buy a work of art," answered Cora.

"You can't invite someone to a work of art!"

"No," said Cora, "but you can invite them to come see it. The statue must be covered up, or something, and people can come watch them uncover it."

But Hailey didn't seem interested in that part of the story. "It's like Cinderella in reverse!" she said now. "The prince dropped his postcard when he ran away. Don't you want to track him down so you can give it back?"

Cora shook her head. "He's probably a mile away by now. And it's just one postcard. He won't miss it." Carefully she tucked the card between two books in her backpack so that it wouldn't get bent.

Hailey gave a fake-romantic sigh. "Your only souvenir of the mysterious Evan."

"Oh stop," said Cora. She was relieved to see her dad's car pulling up. She waved at him, then turned to Hailey. "Want a ride home?"

When the two girls had arranged themselves in the backseat and Cora's father had pulled out of the parking lot, Hailey said, "Okay. So. How did you meet cute, cute Evan?"

Cora gave her a quick explanation, and Hailey nodded in a satisfied way. "Very romantic."

"Is this guy someone I should know about?" asked Cora's father, glancing at Cora in the rearview mirror.

"*Dad!* No! I'm sure I'll never see him again," said Cora.

"He must work at the sculpture garden," suggested Hailey. "It's pretty close by. Have you ever been there?"

"No. I've only heard the name."

Hailey, who was never shy about asking for favors, leaned forward in her seat. "Mr. Nicolaides, could you please drive us past the sculpture garden? Your uneducated daughter has never seen it before."

"Guess I've failed as a parent," said Cora's dad. "Well, it's easy to fix. Sure, I'll take us over that way."

The garden was on a quiet street a few blocks from the girls' school. The house, a dark-red Victorian, was tucked back from the road. Stone paths led to the front door and, from a side door, into the sculpture garden.

Nothing about the house should have been unsettling. It should have looked like the cozy nest it had been built to be. But instead it looked forlorn and neglected. The dark, shaggy shrubs in front hadn't been trimmed in ages. Inside, Cora could see that curtains had been drawn across every window on both floors.

The garden didn't look very welcoming either. Cora hadn't been quite sure what a sculpture garden was. The phrase had made her imagine rows of dignified, regal marble statues, something like what you'd find in the ancient Greek and Roman wing of an art gallery. And "garden"? Of course that called to mind her parents' cheery garden in the backyard. This was nothing like that. The lot was enclosed by an ornate wrought-iron fence that made the statues look like prisoners. Stunted trees had been placed here and there. Apart from them, there was also a tall rectangular hedge—a labyrinth, Hailey said.

The statues Cora could see from the road had been arranged in clusters. They'd been carved out of some kind of grayish stone and made to look like gods, goddesses, and heroes, though here and there Cora spied a few ordinary people from different periods in history. They were *very* realistic. For some reason, Cora didn't enjoy looking at them.

She shuddered a little. "Kind of creepy," she said.

"*Totally* creepy," said Hailey emphatically. "When I was about five, my parents took me here. I don't remember it too well, but my mom says I completely freaked out—they had to take me home. What I don't understand is how anyone could *collect* statues like these."

"There have always been rumors about this place," said Cora's father. "Statues coming to life, strange goings-on in the museum—things like that. All urban legends, but still spooky. I've heard that the garden was built over an old cemetery, and I've also heard that it was built right on top of a fault line. Have you looked at this long enough?"

"Yes!" said both girls in unison.

As Mr. Nicolaides began to drive away from the curb, a branch on one of the nearby trees suddenly shifted position—or at least that was how it looked. Most likely it was the wind. But Cora had the unmistakable impression that an unseen hand had shoved the branch away.

The branch had been concealing the face of the nearest statue. And the expression on the statue's face was terrible.

It was the figure of a woman. She was wearing a tight-fitting buttoned jacket and what looked like a hoop-skirt from the nineteenth century. The clothes had been carved with such amazing skill that the long stone skirt actually seemed to be rippling like fabric. Her hands were covering her eyes to shield them from . . . what?

Whatever it was, it had been something very, very bad. The woman seemed to be twisting away from an invisible tormenter. And her mouth was open in a silent scream of horror.

The car had pulled into traffic now, but Cora couldn't stop staring at that statue's face. Of course it wasn't a real person. Of *course* not. And yet Cora was absolutely certain that the statue was begging for her help.

CHAPTER 2

"It's perfect, Cora. Totally perfect," said Amber.

Cora was staring into the fitting-room mirror of her favorite clothing store at the mall. Hailey, Amber, and Skye were standing behind her.

"You have *got* to get this dress," Amber continued. She looked at the other two friends in the mirror. "You think so too, right?"

"Totally," said Hailey.

"A hundred percent," agreed Skye.

And as she studied her reflection, Cora decided her friends were right. This dress *was* perfect. It was very simple, with a square neckline and cap sleeves. It fit closely down to a flared skirt at the hip line and was made of matte satin in a shade somewhere between blue and lilac. Cora hadn't planned to look at any dresses. What was the point? But when Amber had spotted this one on a sales rack and insisted that Cora had to try it on, she couldn't resist. Besides, it was 20 percent off. . . .

"If I get this, though, it will mean I have to go to the dance," she mused aloud. "Otherwise it will go to waste."

"Of *course* you have to go!" said Hailey. "Did you really think we were going to let you off the hook?"

"And even if you don't have someone . . . um . . . someone specific to go with," added Skye, "in *that* dress you're going to be dancing all night."

Cora spun around and gave her reflection one more look. "Okay! I'll do it!" she said. All of a sudden she felt happy and excited. Maybe she had more in common with her friends than she'd thought. Maybe she could learn to be as outgoing as they were.

For once, why not just relax and stop overthinking?

Which didn't mean Cora wanted to stop thinking about *everything*. Earlier that week she and her friends had been assigned a school project. Now, as they sat in the mall's food court eating ice cream as a reward for all their hard shopping, Cora made an announcement.

"When we get to my house, we're going to do an hour of work first before anything else."

"But it's Saturday," Hailey protested. "*And* it's a sleepover. What kind of hostess are you, making us do homework at a sleepover?"

Cora held firm. "It'll only be for an hour. Then we can order a pizza and *officially* start the sleepover."

"I hate mythology," Amber grumbled. "Why can't we just do a book report like regular people?"

At Cora's school the eighth graders always had a segment on Greek mythology. This year Cora's English teacher had let the kids in class pick their own groups and then told each group to choose one particular myth to study. At the end of the semester each group was going to do some kind of presentation on the myth they'd chosen. Naturally, Cora and her friends had wanted to work together, but they still hadn't decided on their myth.

Cora had gotten a bunch of mythology books out of the library on Tuesday. They were stacked on the coffee table in her living room. When she and her friends got home from the mall, Cora led them into the living room and showed them the books.

"Let's each pick one and see which myths we like."

"Oh, that's not too bad," said a relieved Hailey. "I thought you were going to make us do flash cards or something."

When the girls compared notes a few minutes later, they discovered that each of them wanted to work on a different myth.

"Persephone, definitely," said Cora. "Hades kidnapped her and made her live in the underworld with him."

Skye disagreed. "I like the one about Echo and Narcissus the best. We could have good echo sound effects. And we know *lots* of people who are as conceited as Narcissus."

"What about Eos? She fell in love with this prince— a mortal—and asked the gods to give him eternal life," asked Amber. "But she forgot to ask them to grant him eternal youth. So he lived and lived and got older and older and finally shriveled up into a grasshopper, and she had to keep him in a basket."

"That's probably the weirdest myth I've ever heard," said Hailey. "And besides, you're *all* wrong. We *have* to do King Midas. It's the most famous Greek myth, I'd bet. And it would be fun to show Midas turning things into gold."

"How could we show that?" Cora wondered.

"Oh, we could just use spray paint," Hailey said casually.

Amber frowned. "The story of Midas makes no sense. If everything he touched turned into gold, why didn't *he* turn into gold when he was, like, putting his shoes on? He would have had to touch his feet, right? Or did he wear sandals?"

"You can't look at this kind of thing too closely," said Cora. "*Myths* don't have to work like real life. The point was how stupid his greed made him."

"Who wants to do a myth that has a *point?*" said Skye crossly. "These aren't fables. I don't want to work on something *educational*."

"I'm too hungry to think anymore," said Amber. She clapped her book shut. "Let's order that pizza now. With *no mushrooms*."

"I like mushrooms," Hailey objected. "Let's get half mushroom."

"No way! I'll be able to tell," said Amber. "The flavor will migrate across."

After a marathon debate about extra cheese, onions, sausage versus bacon, and sausage versus no meat at all, the girls decided on two medium pizzas—one for the meat eaters and one with all veggies (but no mushrooms). Cora phoned in the order. All four girls were starving, and the half hour they had to wait seemed endless. When the doorbell rang, they raced for the front door. Cora got there first and yanked the door open.

"*Cora?*" said the boy who was standing on the front steps.

Cora blinked, all pangs of hunger instantly forgotten. "*Evan?*"

Because that's who was at the door—holding two pizza boxes and looking even cuter than she'd remembered.

"What—what are you doing here?" Cora stammered.

Evan seemed surprised by the question. "I have your pizzas. I work at the pizza place around the corner." He held out the two boxes. Wordlessly Cora took them. As the silence stretched on, Hailey gave Cora a hard elbow to the ribs.

"Thanks," she finally managed to say. "Um, see you around, I guess."

"Cora, you have to *pay* him!" Hailey blurted out.

"Oh, that's right! Of course. Sorry. Um, come in for

a second," she told Evan. "I—I have the money right here. Wait, it's in my pocket." Half-dazed, she looked around for a place to set down the pizzas until Amber firmly took them away from her.

"I'll put them in the kitchen," Amber said.

"The kitchen. Right. Okay." Cora was still too rattled to think straight. "Oh! Your money!" She fished the bills out of her pocket and handed them over. "And, um, the tip—"

"No tip." Evan's voice was firm. "No tipping among friends. These are your friends, right?"

Cora introduced him to the three other girls. She couldn't help noticing that they all looked as starstruck as she felt herself. Hailey recovered the fastest. "I've already met you, Evan," she said. "That is, I saw you the other day. You know, when you threw those postcards all over Cora's feet?"

"You don't need to remind me," said Evan, smiling at Cora. "It was a . . . memorable occasion."

Cora was starting to feel more like herself again. "It sure was. What were those—?" Then she realized that Evan was still standing. "Want to sit down?" she added hastily.

"I wish I could, but I shouldn't. The pizza place will need me. I do all the orders that can be delivered on foot around here."

"So the postcards are for a different job?" asked Cora.

"That's a volunteer job," Evan told her. "I work at the sculpture garden on Wednesdays and sometimes Saturdays. They're going to have an unveiling ceremony for a new statue that's coming in a few weeks. The postcards were advertising all the details. When I saw you, I had just dropped off a couple of cards at the middle school office. I was on my way to the post office and then back to the garden when I ran into you. *Literally* ran into you, I mean." He smiled awkwardly.

"We actually passed by the sculpture garden on the way home," said Cora. "I didn't see you there." *Dumb!* she thought instantly. *It's going to sound like I'm stalking him.*

But Evan didn't seem to mind. "I wish I'd been outside so I could've seen you," he said. "But I was in the office sticking address labels onto more postcards. That's the kind of glamorous work I do there. Why don't you come to the garden this Wednesday?" he went on.

For a second Cora thought Evan was talking to all four of them. She felt shivery when she realized that he was looking straight at her. "I can show you around," he said. "It's kind of an interesting place—hey, you're reading Greek myths!" he added suddenly. He had just noticed the library books the girls had stacked on the coffee table. Now he crossed the room to look at them more closely.

"We're supposed to pick a myth to do a project on," explained Cora. "The trouble is, we can't agree on just one."

"They're all pretty great. Which ones are you thinking about?"

"Persephone, Eos and the grasshopper man, Echo and Narcissus—"

"And the *obvious* choice—Midas," interrupted Hailey. "I'm right. Right?"

Evan shrugged. "Midas was okay, I guess. But have you thought about Perseus and Andromeda?"

The girls looked at one another. "We don't quite . . . know who they are," Cora said. "We only just started looking through our books."

"This book's pretty good," Evan said, pointing to the one Cora had used. "This one is too. But this"—he picked up the girls' mythology textbook from the bottom of the pile—"is worthless. The author got everything wrong."

"Wait—what?" said Amber. "What kinds of things did she get wrong?"

"Even the most basic stuff! Dumb little details like saying Actaeon was changed into an elk instead of a stag . . ." Evan's voice trailed off when he realized that all four girls were staring at him. "I just—uh—like Greek myths," he added sheepishly.

"We can tell," said Cora. "So who was Perseus and . . . what was the other one's name?"

Evan brightened. "Andromeda. She was the girl Perseus rescued." He gently took a book off the top of the pile and opened it to the myth. "See," he began, pointing to an illustration. "Perseus was the son of Zeus and a mortal mother, Danaë. He lived on a little island ruled by this kind-of-insane king. When the king announced that he was going to get married, all the guys on the island were supposed to bring him gifts. But Perseus was too poor to come up with a present, so he offered to complete a task instead.

"The king was all over that," Evan continued. "He told Perseus to kill Medusa and bring back her head."

"Medusa was the one with snakes for hair, right?" asked Cora.

"Exactly! She was so horrible-looking that anyone who saw her turned to stone. So Perseus flew to the Gorgons' cave—"

Skye interrupted. "What do you mean, flew? Did he have wings?"

"No, just winged shoes. Plus, Athena gave him a shield that was as bright as a mirror. Hermes gave him—"

"Why was the shield so bright?" broke in Skye for the second time.

"You'll see! So anyway, Hermes gave Perseus this supersharp sword. It could cut through even the hardest metal."

"I don't see why the gods had to make it so easy for Perseus," said Hailey sourly.

Evan shrugged. "The gods play favorites. So *anyway*, Perseus flew to the Gorgons' cave. When he got there, the Gorgons were all sleeping. Perseus looked into the shield instead of looking at them—that's how he kept from turning into stone. He swooped down and lopped off Medusa's head. And that's the story of how Perseus killed Medusa," he finished. "Of course it's more interesting when you read the real myth. I'm leaving out a lot."

"Um, Evan? What about Andromeda?" asked Cora.

Evan smiled. He flipped the page again, but this time it showed a beautiful woman chained to a rock in the sea. "Sorry—didn't mean to leave *her* out! . . . Okay. So on his way home with Medusa's head, Perseus flew over the coast of Ethiopia. He looked down and saw this girl chained to a boulder right at the sea's edge. That was Andromeda. I'm not going to get into how she got there—you'll have to read about it. But the main thing is, this huge sea monster was about to kill her. Perseus killed the monster with his sword, and when Perseus took Andromeda home, he saw her old boyfriend, who hadn't tried to save her, and he used Medusa's head to turn the boyfriend into stone. Then he and Andromeda got married," he finished.

"Wow. I have to admit, there's a lot of good stuff in that myth," said Hailey. "It would be cool to make Medusa's head, for instance."

But Evan wasn't paying attention to Hailey. He had turned back to Cora. "Even if you don't use that myth, you *really* should come to the sculpture garden with me," he told her. "It has a ton of statues from Greek myths. I bet it would help with your project!"

"Probably not," Cora replied regretfully. "How could statues—" She broke off as Hailey punched her in the back.

"I'm *sure* it would help," Hailey said firmly. "And while you're showing Cora around, you can tell her more about the story of Perseus."

This time Evan did listen to Hailey. "She's right," he told Cora. "You owe it to this project to meet me on Wednesday. Also, you owe it to *yourself*. Because I think it would be fun." He flashed his most enchanting smile.

"It would be," Cora agreed. "I—I would love to come, actually." Then she wanted to kick herself. Why had she said "actually" in that dumb way? She hurried on. "Should I meet you there?"

"Why don't we go together?" said Evan easily. "The high school lets out half an hour before the middle school. Want to meet at the car-pool place again? I promise I won't dump postcards on you this time."

"I'll be there," Cora promised. "And thanks."

"Thank you for inviting me in," Evan said gallantly. "But right now I'd better say good-bye. They're going to be wondering what's happened to me."

He turned around when he got to the front door.

"See you Wednesday, Cora. And nice to meet the rest of you."

As soon as the door had closed behind him, Cora's friends burst into screaming laughter.

"*Shhhhhhhhh!*" Cora hissed at them. "He'll hear you!"

But they couldn't stop.

"No, thanks, Prince Charming," Skye said mockingly. "I don't want to go on a date with you because it won't help with our project."

"It's not a date! He's just showing me where he works, is all."

"Okay, fine," said Skye. "But what were you *thinking?*"

"I know, I know. My brain wasn't working," Cora confessed.

"It sure wasn't," Skye told her emphatically. "You're lucky Hailey saved you. Evan seems really nice. Plus he's better-looking than Adonis!"

"Wait." Amber sounded puzzled. "Who's Adonis?"

"Adonis was this amazingly handsome Greek guy," Hailey told her. "You'd know about him if you'd been paying attention in class yesterday. But you're right, Skye. He's really. Really. Really. Cute."

"Who—Adonis?" said Amber.

"No, *Evan!*" said the other three girls in unison.

"Cute *and* an older man," Skye put in slyly. "This is going to be the talk of the school next week."

"Stop! He's just a year older than we are," said Cora. "Don't make such a big thing out of it."

"Cora. Look me in the eye," ordered Hailey. "A super-good-looking high school guy just asked you out on a date, pretty much. How about just being happy?"

But Cora was already happy. Very, very happy.

All through dinner, and the movie they'd ordered on demand, and the late-night talking (until Cora's mom told them to be quiet), and then the whispering until one by one the girls dropped off to sleep—through all of that, Cora kept wanting to pinch herself to make sure this was really happening. Happening to her, the girl who twenty-four hours before had been feeling so sorry for herself about being left out.

She didn't want to fall asleep, because then she'd stop thinking about Evan. On the other hand, the sooner she did fall asleep, the sooner the next morning would come when she could think about him again.

And Cora was pretty sure she would dream about him. . . .

CHAPTER 3

No matter how late she fell asleep, Cora was usually the first person awake at a sleepover. Of course, that had something to do with sleeping on the floor instead of in a nice comfortable bed, but she was also a morning person. Often she'd read in her sleeping bag for what felt like hours before her friends slowly came back to consciousness. But not at *this* sleepover. Cora had been so churned up by seeing Evan again that she didn't fall asleep properly until about five a.m. It wasn't until Hailey whomped her with a pillow to the head the next morning that she finally opened her eyes a crack.

"Why are you hitting me?" Cora croaked. "Leave me alone."

"No! Get up, get up, get up! We've been awake for *three hours!*" said Hailey. "We want some breakfast before our parents come to get us."

"You don't need me for that," Cora said, shutting her eyes again. "You know where everything in my kitchen is. Go get your own breakfasts."

"I already had some cereal," said Amber. "I'm hungry again."

"And Skye and I haven't had a bite," said Hailey. "C'mon, Cora. Get up! You're going to need lots of energy."

"Why?" grumbled Cora.

"So you'll survive until Wednesday when you see Evan. Why else?"

Evan! At the sound of his name Cora bolted upright and scrambled out of her sleeping bag. How could she have forgotten him for a single second, even while she'd been sleeping?

"Well, *that* worked," Skye observed. "Sorry if we took you away from dreaming about Evan."

Now Cora saw that her friends were not only wide awake but dressed, with their sleeping bags rolled up. She couldn't believe she'd slept through it all. "I don't remember dreaming about anything," she said as she quickly got dressed. "Maybe my brain was too worn out from thinking about Evan while I was still awake. That all really did happen, right? I mean, he brought our pizza and asked me to go to the sculpture garden and—"

"And you dumbly said no, but I came to your rescue?" interrupted Hailey. "Yes. It all happened. And now that you're up, can we have breakfast?"

To Cora it felt as though Wednesday would never get there. But Wednesday had no choice. No matter how slowly Monday and Tuesday crawled along, it still had to follow. And no matter how extra slowly the school day dragged on Wednesday, it still had to end. Cora wasn't sure whether she was more excited or more nervous about spending the afternoon with Evan. Both made the pit of her stomach feel exactly the same.

"Come to the car-pool area with me," she begged Hailey when school let out.

"Why?" asked her friend. "Evan won't want *me* tagging along."

"Just keep me company in case he's late, okay? I

mean, what if he stands me up? What if he was just kidding around on Saturday?"

"Cora, *relax*. He's gonna be there."

And sure enough, Evan was already waiting for her when they arrived. "Time for me to melt out of sight," murmured Hailey. She gave Evan a cheerful wave. "Hi! And good-bye," she called. She took a few deliberate steps backward. Then, still looking at Evan and Cora, she slowly walked sideways until she had vanished behind some shrubbery.

"What was *that* all about?" asked Evan.

Cora giggled. "I think that's what Hailey calls 'melting out of sight.' You know, discreetly leaving us alone."

"So that's what being discreet looks like," said Evan. "Funny, I always though it meant trying *not* to attract attention." He gestured toward three sixth graders who were openly staring at Hailey's progress behind the bushes.

"So how do you like visiting your old school?" Cora asked as they headed for the sidewalk.

"Huh?" Evan asked, looking puzzled. "Oh, I actually didn't go to this middle school. We just moved here over the summer."

"From where?"

"Oh, all over the place. My dad's in the army. He gets moved a lot."

"Well, where did you go?" persisted Cora.

"It was a very small middle school in a very small town in Pennsylvania."

"How small? I mean, how small was the school?"

"It's not like I have an exact count. About forty kids per grade, I guess."

"Wow, that *is* small. Compared to here, was it more fun or less?"

Evan turned to smile at her. "It's definitely more fun here," he said. "The girls are much nicer. Now let me fill you in on the sculpture garden.

"I've been volunteering there for a couple of months. The place is run by two sisters who are my bosses. There's Eunice—she's older, I think, but it's kind of hard to tell. And then the other one is Stesha. Their last name is Metaxas, so you can probably figure out how the garden got its name. The museum is on the first floor of their house, along with their office. The museum's got mostly small stuff—coins, jewelry, things like that. The garden is the main attraction."

"Metaxas sounds like a Greek last name," said Cora.

"I'm Greek and my grandparents were from Greece, so I notice stuff like that."

"You're right! The sisters moved here from Greece too, but I don't know when, exactly. Someone in their family made a pile of money and left it to them. Eunice and Stesha used the money to start the Metaxas Sculpture Garden. And there's enough money left over to keep it going pretty much forever."

"It didn't look as if anyone was there when my dad drove us past the garden a few days ago," said Cora.

"Yeah, it doesn't bring in much of a crowd. There's enough money that the sisters don't really care about getting people in. But with this new statue they're unveiling, they may get more visitors than usual."

Cora and Evan had reached a busy corner now. As they waited for the light to change, Cora asked, "What's the new statue of? Or who's it supposed to be—or however you're supposed to ask that?"

"It's going to be Andromeda, actually," said Evan.

"Oh! Is that why you thought of her the other night at my house?"

"I guess so." Evan sounded distracted. "When's this light going to change? Oh, there it goes. *Finally*." He strode across the street so briskly that Cora had to hurry to keep up.

When they'd crossed the street, she said, "I've reread the myth a couple of times—we're definitely going to do our English project on it. But one thing I don't get: Why would Andromeda want to marry someone who had turned her boyfriend to stone?"

Evan turned to look at her in amazement. "Andromeda's boyfriend didn't do a thing to help her! He ran away when he saw the monster," he said, sounding almost angry. "What a coward."

"Isn't that a little extreme?" said Cora. "If I saw a sea monster, I don't think I'd stick around either."

Evan sighed. "You're right. I'm sorry."

In Cora's opinion, Evan had nothing to be sorry about. Maybe he was like Cora and got really into whatever he was reading. Sometimes Cora got so involved in a book that it started to seem more alive than the real world. Sometimes she even—

"Uh, Cora? We're here."

Cora laughed and ran back to Evan. "Oh! I didn't even notice—I was thinking about something."

They had reached the dark-red Victorian house. As

they headed down the walkway, Evan said, "Let's skip the museum today." He lowered his voice. "It's not that interesting."

"Are the sisters in there now?"

"Probably," said Evan, "but they won't mind my bringing a guest. In fact, they'll probably be glad to see fresh blood. . . . Just kidding," he added with a wink, seeing Cora's startled glance. "I mean, they'll be glad to have a young visitor for a change. But you can meet them another time. Let me show you the sculpture garden."

An elaborate, dark wrought-iron gate marked the entrance. Evan swung it open with a flourish. "After you, mademoiselle!"

Cora knew that her imagination sometimes went into overdrive. She also knew that first impressions weren't always right. Still, she was positive that when she walked through the gate, the air became a little colder. And it wasn't only the cold that made her shiver. The garden's whole atmosphere seemed somehow *wrong*. The shade under the trees looked darker, and the grass seemed gray—as if all the color had been drained from the world. The labyrinth in the middle of the lawn loomed up like a fortress. And the sculptures . . .

Her father had mentioned a rumor about the sculpture garden being built over an old graveyard. Was that why the statues suddenly looked like tombstones to Cora?

Oh, stop, she told herself. *The statues look like statues.* But not the kind of statue you felt like lingering in front of.

"The sculptures are all so . . . anguished-looking," she said to Evan. "Everyone is either sad or scared!"

Evan laughed. "That's what the sisters go for. They like what they call 'powerful emotions caught in stone.'"

"'Caught' in stone? *Trapped* is more like it!" Cora was studying the statue of a man who was stretching out his hands as if he were begging for mercy. "This poor guy! What's his problem? And the woman over there—she looks as if she's trying to pull a blanket over her head. Isn't there even one statue of a cute little girl carrying a basket of flowers?"

"The garden can get to you after a while," Evan agreed. "But there are some cool animals. Look at that gigantic wild boar. And the peacock is cool."

The stone peacock was more than cool—it was amazing. Its tail had been carved with incredible attention to detail, and each feather looked as weightless as the real thing.

"How could the sculptor make a stone bird look so light?" marveled Cora. "You'd think it could fly away if it wanted to."

"I know what you mean. Look up at that tree." Evan pointed to the branch of a nearby tree where a stone eagle had been perched. The bird looked so ready to pounce that Cora flinched at the first sight of it.

"Remember how on Saturday I told you there were some statues from Greek mythology here? Let's go see those," said Evan. He grinned down at her. "Because we want this visit to be *educational*, right?"

"Oh, absolutely. We're *all* about education. That one over there—isn't that Artemis?"

"Yup. And there's her bow and arrow. The myths say she would point at a leaf on a tree and then shoot an arrow right through the center of it. She was amazing."

Cora pointed. "And there's Ares, looking cranky."

As they passed Ares, Evan continued talking about the statues as if they were old friends. "He always had his shield with him," Evan said. "Of course, wars did usually start wherever he went. I guess that's what happens when you're the god of war."

"This must be Aphrodite." Cora gestured toward the

statue of a beautiful young woman standing in a seashell.

"Yup. And Hephaestus!" Evan clapped a familiar hand onto the shoulder of the statue they were passing just then. "Hey, buddy! How're you doing?"

Cora laughed. "Do you like talking to statues?" she said teasingly.

"Just the ones I know," he answered. He pointed to a winding pebble path. "That's where we're headed."

At the end of the path, rearing up in front of them, was a huge centaur.

Cora shivered. "That guy is *massive*. Look at those shoulders. They must be—" She broke off as she caught sight of another statue. "Ewww. Is that a harpy?"

"Yup," said Evan. "Bird body, woman's head. Not as impressive as the centaur, somehow."

He was right. The harpy's low-slung, stocky body had the shape of a clumsy duck, and its human head looked as if it had been screwed onto the duck's shoulders. Still, the statue managed to be shockingly realistic. The woman's mouth was open in an angry scream that even showed a couple of missing teeth.

"You'd think that the artist worked from life except for the fact that there's no such thing as a harpy," said

Cora. "And I'm glad there isn't. This thing is *horrible*. Hey, what happened over there?" She had just noticed a spot about twenty feet away where an empty pedestal stood. Without waiting for Evan's answer, Cora walked over to look.

Attached to the pedestal was a bronze plaque. PERSEUS, it read.

Cora turned to Evan, who had just caught up to her. "Where'd he go?"

"I'm not sure," said Evan. "Maybe they took the statue away for cleaning."

"Wouldn't it make more sense to clean it here?"

Evan shrugged. For some reason he looked very uncomfortable.

"Maybe he flew off to look for Andromeda," Cora joked.

It wasn't the quip of the century, she realized. Still, there was no reason for Evan to whip around and ask, "What do you mean?" He shot a quick glance over his shoulder, but of course no one was there. "It probably just needed repairing. Hey, would you like to go in the labyrinth?" He gestured toward the far end of the garden at what had once been a severely clipped boxwood hedge about ten feet tall. Now the boxwood looked shaggy and overgrown, as if no one had tended to it for a long time.

"Will we be able to find our way out?"

"Oh yeah. I've walked that labyrinth so many times that I know the path by heart. Think of this as your personal guided tour."

The entrance to the boxwood maze was the only part that didn't confuse Cora. The minute she and Evan stepped into the labyrinth, they were faced with what looked like a solid wall of hedging.

"Aren't you supposed to start with a path?" she asked.

Evan grinned. "Oh, there's a path. You just have to find it."

"All I see is this hedge!"

"I didn't say it was easy," Evan teased her. Taking her hand, he led her toward the left end of the hedge.

He's holding my hand. He's actually holding my hand!

Cora lost her breath for a second, so flabbergasted that she stopped watching where she was going. She stumbled on a stray root and would have fallen if Evan hadn't steadied her.

"Easy there," he said.

Instantly Cora felt blood rush to her face. What if

Evan was only holding her hand so she wouldn't trip? She'd better not get too excited.

The slightest sliver of a door had been cut through the boxwood ahead of them. It was so narrow that she and Evan had to scrape through sideways. How did he know which way to turn? In some places the hedge walls were so overgrown that she and Evan were practically crashing through the bushes rather than following a path. And Evan led her around so many corners that it seemed as though they were walking in circles instead of making any progress. But after just a few minutes they reached the cool, quiet center of the maze . . . where a huge stone Minotaur was sitting on a rocky throne as if he had been waiting for them all this time.

"*Whoa,*" said Cora. "He is *way* too realistic." She shivered. "But it's cool to have a real Minotaur at the center of a labyrinth. A statue of one, anyway."

"So you know the Minotaur, too!" Evan sounded pleased.

Cora laughed. "A guy with the body of a man and the head of a bull? Trapped in the middle of a labyrinth in the dungeon of a king's castle? Once you've heard about the Minotaur, you don't forget him."

"I don't know if I'd call a man-eating monster a 'guy,'" Evan objected as he led Cora through a shortcut that got them out of the labyrinth quickly. "But I'm glad you know who he is. You must've really been studying since Saturday. Anyway, enough education. Want to play hide-and-seek?"

Cora stared at him. "Just the two of us?"

"What's wrong with that?"

"Nothing, I guess," Cora said after a second. She was surprised that he'd suggested a game that seemed so babyish, but Cora felt a rush of butterflies in her stomach at the thought of Evan finding her. . . .

"Okay—you hide. I'll seek. I'll count to fifty."

"Not fifty! A hundred!" Cora objected. "You know this place way better than I do."

"A hundred, then. But one thing: We have to be careful. Eunice and Stesha are working in their offices. They wouldn't like us crashing around all these priceless statues."

"They're made of stone! How could we hurt them?"

"Some of them are fragile," Evan told her. "Some are hollow, for one thing. And the sisters would be mad if we even scratched them."

"Okay. I promise not to crash around," said Cora solemnly.

"Here we go, then." Evan turned his back to lean against a tree and cover his eyes. "One, two—can you hear me okay?"

"Yes."

"Okay. One, two, three . . ."

Cora stole off as quickly and quietly as she could. If she stayed off the worn paths and on the grass, Evan wouldn't be able to hear which way she was going. Quickly she surveyed the sculpture garden. The challenge in a place like this was that since there were no walls, you could be hunted from all sides.

Going back into the labyrinth would be too obvious and too hard for her on her own. What about that woman with the umbrella? She was wearing a long, billowing skirt that would be good to hide behind. But that would also be an obvious spot. Some of the trees looked climbable, but they'd rustle while she was going up—and the sisters definitely wouldn't like it if she broke a branch.

You're overthinking again, Cora scolded herself. *This is a game, not a contest. You don't have to strategize—just pick a fun place to hide. . . .*

47

Like the statue of the girl over there, the one staring up. She looked to be about Cora's age and was pretty much her same size. She wasn't mounted on a pedestal. What if Cora stood behind her, in the same position? Evan might not notice her at first, and at least it would be a creative way to hide.

Cora dashed over to the stone girl and positioned her arms and legs in exactly the same way as the statue. Then she settled herself to wait.

"Ready or not, here I come!" she heard Evan call. Cora smiled to herself. She was ready!

A couple of silent minutes passed. Cora couldn't hear footsteps. The stone was making her cold. She hoped this wouldn't take much longer. . . .

Cora jumped a little as she heard a low sound nearby. Carefully she steadied herself back into her hiding pose. But now she was listening tensely. What was that sound?

A hissing, swishing noise, broken by brief pauses. Almost like words. But who could be speaking out here? And wasn't there more than one voice? Cora tried to listen even more closely. The sounds seemed to be all around her now, hovering just out of range. They were definitely coming from more than one place.

Ghostly voices in the wind, Cora found herself thinking. She shivered and pressed herself harder against the back of the statue.

Cora felt the movement before she saw it. The stone shook the tiniest bit and then shifted position slightly.

This time Cora jumped back, looking wildly around. Her dad had mentioned a fault line. Was this the beginning of an earthquake?

But nothing else happened. The ground was still; the statue was still. Cora glanced around the garden. Everything she could see was motionless.

Yet something felt different. Or was it that something *looked* different?

Cora looked at the statue of the girl again. It was fixed in the same position except for one thing. When she had first spotted it, its head had been staring up.

Now the statue was staring down and back, as if trying to see what was behind it. It was looking at Cora.

CHAPTER 4

A few times, in nightmares, Cora had woken herself up by screaming. The sound had been embarrassing—more like a strangled squeal than a full-blooded shriek. But now, when someone suddenly grabbed her from behind, Cora had no trouble screaming full out.

"It's me! It's me!" came Evan's voice. "I was just tagging you."

Cora could feel her whole body relax a little, but she was still shaking as struggled to get to her feet. "You scared me," she said.

"Yeah, I can see that," Evan answered. "But you made it too easy. Why weren't you hiding?" Then he looked closely at Cora. "Hey, what's wrong?"

Cora swallowed. "You're not—you're not going to believe me. But it happened. It really did!"

"What did?"

Cora pointed a shaking hand at the statue of the girl next to them. "Sh-she's looking at me! Before, she was staring up."

Confused, Evan glanced around. "Wait. Who's looking at you?"

"The statue." Cora paused, realizing how ridiculous that sounded. "I know it's insane. But she wasn't looking at me before."

Evan looked up at the sky. "It's getting foggy. You must've seen some mist blowing by that made you *think* the statue had moved."

But Cora was insistent. "Fog wouldn't make me think she had shifted her head! Anyway, I felt her move before I saw her. I thought it was an earthquake at first."

"That would make more sense," Evan said. "I didn't feel anything, but it could've been one of those quakes that are too small to measure." He sounded very sure of himself now. "It had to have been something like that. Because this statue's head has always been facing the same way."

"Not true!"

Evan shook his own head. "Cora, I've been in this garden at least thirty or forty times. I know every statue here. I'm telling you, this girl has always been looking down and back." He tapped the statue a couple of times. "Maybe what you felt was the stone cracking somewhere. Although it looks okay to me."

Cora sighed. Evan had to be right. And yet at the same time, she felt *positive* that the statue had moved.

She stared at the stone girl. The statue's opaque gray eyes stared blindly back.

"My turn to hide," said Evan. "Are you ready?"

But whatever fun the game had held was gone for Cora. No way did she want to prowl around this garden alone. "I don't think I—"

"Cora! Over here!"

A few minutes earlier Cora would have been disappointed to see her mom's car pulling into the garden entrance to take her home. Now she was relieved. This thing with the statue was really bothering her. She wanted to go back to normal life even if it meant homework and chores.

"Coming!" she called, waving back at her mother.

"Any chance you'd like to help me this Saturday?"

Evan asked quickly. "I have to get out more invitations for the unveiling of the new statue."

Cora paused. "I'd like to see you, but inside. Not out here."

"I understand," Evan replied. "The garden *is* kind of creepy. I guess I've just gotten used to it. But this would start at six o'clock. I have to work at the pizza place all afternoon. So no garden—we'll just be sitting in a conference room."

This sounded more like a real date. Cora said, "I think I can handle a conference room. I'll need to check with my parents, though. Want me to text you?"

"Why go to the trouble? Can we ask your mom right now?"

Seconds later Cora was introducing Evan to her mother.

"It's not much of a date," Evan told Mrs. Nicolaides. (He had called it a date! Now it was official!) "But if Cora's up for it, it would sure help me a lot. My bosses will both be there if we need chaperoning."

Mrs. Nicolaides was checking her calendar. "Cora's dad and I aren't doing anything on Saturday. We can bring her and pick her up."

Evan's face brightened. "Great! Thanks a lot, Mrs. Nicolaides." He turned to Cora. "I'll bring a pizza from work. What do you want on it?"

"Anything except meat. Especially anchovies."

"I love anchovies," said Evan. "But for you, I'll give them up."

"Also no green peppers. Red ones are okay, though."

"At least we agree about that," said Evan. "Okay, I think I can remember all this. See you Saturday night. Good to have met you," he added to Cora's mother.

Mrs. Nicolaides smiled warmly at him. "You too, Evan. See you soon."

"He seems nice," she told Cora as the car pulled out into traffic.

"He is," Cora said after a second.

"Everything okay, honey?"

"Oh! Yep."

But as Cora and her mom made their way through the town and back home, Cora couldn't shake the terrifying moment with the sculpture from her mind. It really hadn't moved. Had it?

Evan was waiting on the front steps of the museum. He jumped to his feet when he saw her.

"I know I promised we'd be working inside," he said. "But it's been such a nice day, and it's still light out. Wouldn't you like to work in the garden after all? At least until it gets dark?"

"Okay," said Cora after a second. It *was* beautiful out, and they'd be together—and anyway, what could happen? The more she thought about it, the more Cora had persuaded herself that the statue couldn't possibly have turned its head. Things like that *just didn't happen.*

"Great! I've got the invitations right here." Evan gestured toward the box on the steps. "We can sit on that bench over by the river nymph."

The river nymph was a statue, of course. Again, the sculptor had carved her with amazing realism. Cora could practically feel the water streaming from the nymph's long hair. Somehow, too, Cora could tell that the nymph had just stepped out of the water. She didn't look as scared as some of the statues in the garden, although she did have a startled expression. But maybe that was supposed to be realistic too. After all, a water nymph might be just as surprised to see a human as the other way around. *I guess it does make sense,* Cora thought.

She and Evan sat side by side on the bench, and he pulled out a pile of envelopes. "These need address labels," he told Cora. "Labels which I . . . don't see in this box." He shuffled the paper in the box around a bit. "I must've left them inside. I'll run in and get them."

Cora jumped to her feet. "Wait!" she called. "I'll come too!" But Evan had already disappeared inside the museum.

A cloud slid over the sun, and Cora shivered. How could one cloud turn the air so much colder?

And how could that fog be coming on so fast? The sun had been shining brightly just a few seconds ago. Now the garden was wreathed in low-lying patches of damp, clammy mist so thick that Cora could barely see the statues around her.

An icy drop of water ran down the back of Cora's neck. Then another. She glanced up. To her horror, the face of the water nymph was now only inches from her own. The nymph's skin was gray stone. Her carved eyes were blank and blind. But her granite curls were dripping real water.

Cora heard a splash and saw that the nymph was now

standing in a spreading pool of water. Was it raining? No, the water was pouring off the nymph herself, drenching the ground under her. It was getting deeper and deeper. Cora could feel it splashing against her own feet. Then it reached her ankles. The pool was becoming a whirlpool now. Cora could feel the current around her legs.

The nymph reached out and pressed her cold, heavy hands onto Cora's shoulders. She was pushing Cora toward the center of the whirlpool. . . .

Where was Evan? Wild with terror, Cora looked toward the museum. There he was—standing outside the gate and staring at her.

"She's going to drown me!" she screamed. But incredibly, he was farther away. His eyes locked on hers, he was stepping backward toward the building. He was going to leave her alone.

Now she realized that Evan had left her with the nymph on purpose.

Cora struggled as hard as she could, but there was no escaping the nymph's icy grip. In a second it would all be over. . . .

"Cora! Cora! Honey, wake up!"

As she rose out of the water and her nightmare,

Cora realized that the hands on her shoulders were her mother's. Her mom was gently shaking her awake. She wasn't in a whirlpool—this was her own bed at home.

"Mom," Cora said groggily, struggling to sit up. "I'm glad it's you."

"You were screaming in your sleep," her mother told her. "Really screaming. You must have been having a terrible dream."

Cora rubbed the sleep from her eyes. "I was. What . . . what day is it?"

"It's still Wednesday, honey," said her mother. "For a few more minutes, anyway. It's almost midnight. Dad and I were on our way to bed when we heard you."

Cora flopped back down with relief. It really hadn't happened. Saturday hadn't come yet. Evan hadn't tricked her. Everything was fine.

Cora turned onto her stomach and snuggled down under the covers. Her mom got up and turned out the light. "Thanks, Mom," Cora murmured. "G'night."

But as Cora tossed and turned, she realized getting back to sleep wouldn't be quite as easy as she hoped. She couldn't get the image of the granite nymph with stone eyes out of her mind.

"All right, people. Let's talk about the reading for today," Ms. Finch announced during first-period English class the next morning.

Cora had done the reading, but she didn't want to be the first to raise her hand. She always tried to ration her hand raising throughout the school day to keep from looking like a show-off. Along with the rest of the class, she sat motionless and hoped Ms. Finch wouldn't call on her.

"Cora? What can you tell us about Perseus? I know your team's been working on that story."

Oh well, Cora thought.

"Perseus was the son of Zeus and a mortal woman named Danaë," Cora began. "Danaë's father, Acrisius, had been told that his daughter's son would grow up to kill him, so when Perseus was born, Acrisius decided to kill *him* first. But then he found out that Zeus was the father of Perseus. He was scared to kill Zeus's son, so he put Perseus and Danaë into a trunk and had the trunk thrown into the ocean. He figured that if they died, Zeus would blame it on Poseidon, the god of the sea."

"It was an evil deed." Ms. Finch used her admonishing voice, as if she were warning the class not to try the same trick with their own relatives. "Go on, Cora."

"So anyway, Zeus made the trunk float to an island. A fisherman rescued Danaë and Perseus and took them in. And . . . and . . ." Cora stopped to suppress a yawn. She had gone back to sleep an hour or so after her nightmare, but it hadn't been a sound sleep. She'd woken up a couple of times and had finally decided to get up for good at five. Her head wasn't nearly as clear as usual.

She swallowed another yawn. "So Perseus found a princess named Andromeda chained to a rock in the middle of the ocean. And he—"

"Wait a second, Cora," Ms. Finch broke in. "You're jumping ahead. What happened before Perseus rescued Andromeda?"

"Oops. He killed Medusa."

"Is Medusa the one with snakes for hair?" asked a boy in the class.

"Yes, Liam," said Ms. Finch with heavy patience. "As I'm sure you remember *from your reading*, Medusa was the one with snakes for hair. Do you remember another unusual thing about her?"

60

"Um . . . she was ugly?" ventured Liam.

"*Very* ugly. So ugly that anyone who looked at her turned to stone. And the king of the island where Perseus lived gave him the task of slaying Medusa."

Ms. Finch turned and wrote PERSEUS SLAYS MEDUSA on the board.

"Ms. Finch, why do myths always say stuff like 'slay' instead of 'kill'?" asked Hailey.

Good question, Cora thought drowsily. She yawned again. Then she pinched her forearm as hard as she could, hoping that the pain would make her more alert. But that only worked for as long as the pinch lasted. Cora shifted restlessly in her seat, twisting her head and shoulders to stretch her cramped neck.

And as she was twisting to the right, she saw someone peering through the window in the classroom door.

Evan.

No one else in the class seemed to have noticed, and Ms. Finch had her back to the door. The only person who saw him was Cora. Her heart started beating faster at the sight of him, but as she looked at his face, the fluttery feelings disappeared.

Why did she suddenly feel scared?

It's Evan, Cora told herself. *Not some bad guy.*

Still, his expression made him look completely different from the Evan she knew. His eyes were coldly darting back and forth as if he were searching for someone. And that someone could only be herself.

Cora felt as if she were pinned to her chair waiting to be caught.

And then his eyes locked on hers.

CHAPTER 5

Cora jumped to her feet so fast that she knocked over her chair. But the instant she moved, Evan's face disappeared from the little window.

"Are you all right, Cora?" asked Ms. Finch.

Everyone in the class was staring at her.

"I—I'm fine," Cora said sheepishly as she picked up her chair and sat down again. "I just—uh—I thought I saw a bee."

"A *bee*? Where?" That came from Randi Abelson, who could be counted on to have hysterics whenever she got the chance. "I think I'm allergic to bee stings! Can I go to the nurse's office?"

"Calm down, Randi," said Ms. Finch. "There's no bee."

"But Cora saw one!"

"I *thought* I saw one," said Cora. "I was wrong. Sorry, everyone."

The imaginary bee had done its work. No one was thinking about Cora now.

That was lucky, she said to herself as the class settled down again. But was she going crazy? Evan couldn't have been at the window. What would he be doing out of school at nine in the morning? And even if he *had* been out of school for some reason, why would he have come to the middle school?

And if, just possibly, he had somehow come to the middle school because he wanted to see her, then why had he been staring at her in that strange, expressionless way?

Since none of those things could have happened, it followed that Evan hadn't been at the window. Cora's busy imagination had tripped her up again.

Why had she been seeing things these last few days? It had to be because she was tired. *I've got to get to bed early tonight,* Cora thought with another yawn.

"What's up with you, Cora?" Skye asked at lunch. "Have you heard anything I've been saying?"

Cora looked blankly at her friend. "Have you been talking?"

Cora, Hailey, Amber, and Skye were at their usual lunch table. They had been there for—Cora checked the wall clock—fifteen minutes. And in all that time, Cora might as well have been on the moon.

She forced a smile. "Sorry, Skye. I was thinking about something else."

"Obviously," said Skye. "Because if you'd been paying attention, you would have known that in about two minutes, Caleb Lasser is going to be coming over here to ask you something. He told me so this morning."

"Ask *me* something? What do you—"

"Shhh," squealed Amber. "He's coming this way!"

Cora didn't know Caleb well, but he was one of the cutest guys in the eighth grade. She'd had an on-and-off crush on him for a couple of years. As he walked toward the girls' table now, though, Cora wasn't getting the same sort of floaty feeling she usually got when she was around him. *Maybe it's just because I'm still tired,* Cora thought.

Her friends were suddenly finding their food tremendously interesting. All three of them were staring fixedly down at their lunches. What was going on?

"Hi, Cora," said Caleb, smiling at her as he smoothed back his blond hair.

"Hi," answered Cora.

"I was wondering if you had any plans for the dance."

"Plans?" echoed Cora.

"Well, yeah. I mean, do you want to go with me?"

"Oh, *that* dance! Um—thanks, Caleb." She took a deep breath in and stared down at her mythology book. "But I can't."

Her three friends whipped around to stare at her. "What do you mean, you can't?" asked Hailey.

"I—I guess I didn't tell you," Cora faltered. "I'm planning on going with someone else. With Evan, actually."

"No, you certainly didn't tell us." Skye sounded annoyed. "That's why I told Caleb you'd say yes."

Caleb was looking from Cora to Skye, confused. "Who's Evan?" asked Caleb.

"Just a friend," said Cora.

Maybe Caleb wasn't used to having girls turn him down. He didn't seem to have brought a plan for being refused. For a few awkward seconds, no one knew where to look. Then Caleb slowly said, "Okay, then. Thanks anyway, I guess. See you around."

As soon as Caleb was out of earshot, Hailey asked, "Are you really going to the dance with Evan?"

"Sort of," said Cora groggily. "I'm planning to ask him . . . soon. . . ."

"Why didn't you *tell* us?" Skye sounded indignant.

"Well, I haven't actually *asked* him yet."

"Asked him yet" was an understatement—Cora hadn't even *mentioned* the dance to Evan yet! But somehow, in that moment Cora realized that she'd already made up her mind to ask Evan. Evan was cute and hardworking and smart. He cared about volunteering, and he liked to talk about books and mythology—things that she was sure Caleb Lasser had never thought twice about.

I'm going with Evan, or I'm going alone, Cora suddenly vowed to herself. *Now I just have to convince him to say yes.*

When Saturday night finally came, Cora still hadn't mentioned the dance to Evan. She'd felt so bold in the lunchroom on Thursday, but as she walked up the path to the museum's front door, Cora's excitement disappeared. With every step she took toward the monstrous house, a bit of happiness drained out of her.

A note was taped to the museum's front door.

C—

I'm in the first room on the right—the one with the lion outside. Come on in!

—E

Cora took the note and pushed open the heavy front door. She found herself in a large lobby that would have been elegant if it hadn't been crammed with vases, urns, and animal sculptures. What looked like a forest of them covered much of the floor and the entire reception desk. They were even precariously piled against the room's tall windows. It was easy to see that the Metaxas sisters had another whole collection, one that could have filled its own sculpture garden.

Cora threaded her way through the animals until

she reached a long hallway. The lights weren't up all the way, but she could see four closed doors on each side. A smallish stone lion was poised to spring outside the first door on the right.

Cora knocked on the heavy door.

"Evan?"

There was no answer. She knocked again, then pushed the door open.

The room was dark and empty. Evan wasn't there.

Maybe he was just late? But no, he'd left that note for her. Maybe he was in the garden. Cora didn't love the idea of going out there at dusk, but waiting in this empty room might be worse. She could hear slow footsteps overhead. Was one of Evan's bosses coming downstairs?

It's okay for me to be here, Cora reminded herself. Still, she didn't feel like meeting either of the Metaxas sisters without Evan.

Well, she had come to see Evan, and she was going to see Evan! Squaring her shoulders, Cora walked briskly down the hall and out the front door.

It wasn't dark out yet, but the day was winding down. The statues in the garden looked pale and ghostly in the half dusk. Cora was glad there was a flashlight on her phone if she needed it. If it got dark, she didn't want to be passing by those silent stone figures alone.

Standing by the entrance gate, she called Evan's name. The garden was silent except for the song of one drowsy bird somewhere.

Cora tried again. "Evan?"

Wherever he was, he didn't answer. So Cora took a deep breath and walked into the garden.

It was a quiet, windless evening—but all around her Cora could hear rustling and what sounded like murmurs. *It's just birds going to bed,* she told herself firmly. *Or squirrels.*

Or the statues coming to life.

Stop, Cora ordered herself. If she wasn't careful, she'd start thinking she was surrounded by giant spiders. Everything was fine!

No one's hand had grazed her shoulder just then. No one was breathing. No one was whispering. No one suddenly *stopped* whispering when she walked by.

"Evan?" Cora called in what she hoped were clear, ringing tones.

There was still no answer. But when Cora turned the corner, there he was.

He was sitting cross-legged on the ground, staring with dull eyes at the empty pedestal where the Perseus statue had been.

"*Evan!* I've been looking everywhere for you! How could you not have heard me?"

Evan gave a start and jumped to his feet. "Hey, Cora! Where'd you come from?"

"From the museum," Cora said. "You weren't in the conference room, so I thought you might be out here. And so . . . here you are," she finished lamely.

Evan rubbed his eyes. "What time is it?"

Cora checked her phone. "Quarter after six."

"Wow. I'm really sorry! I—uh—it was getting stuffy inside, so I came out for some fresh air. I guess I must've dozed off."

"Dozed off? Sitting up with your eyes open?"

Even chuckled weakly. "I don't know. I was thinking about a lot of things."

"I guess so," said Cora. "I called your name three times and you didn't answer."

Evan gave himself a little shake as if to pull himself together. "Can I get a do-over? I'll go inside and wait for you. Then you can come in and find me."

Cora couldn't help laughing. "That's okay," she said. "I don't mind going in together."

"I'm sorry. And I'm also starving. Let's heat up the pizza before we do anything else," Evan said as they crossed the lawn. "It's in the office kitchen. So I got *one* thing right, anyway."

Cora was relieved to see that the little kitchen was delightfully normal-looking—not sparkling clean, but at least it wasn't filled with stone alligators. Evan had already put the pizza on a baking sheet. Now all he had to do was put it into the oven and get two sodas from the refrigerator. Then they sat down to wait for the few minutes it would take the pizza to heat through.

"I have kind of a weird question," Cora said. "You didn't, um, come to my school on Thursday, did you?"

Evan looked surprised. "Of course not. Why?"

"It's just that I thought I saw you looking in the door of my English class."

"What? That's impossible. I have geometry class then. Anyway, why would I do that?"

"I don't know! I said it was a weird question."

"Maybe *you* dozed off," Evan suggested teasingly.

That was probably what had happened, Cora knew,

especially with how little sleep she'd been getting lately. But now something else was nagging at her. What was it? Something Evan had just said. Cora tried to retrace her thoughts. Weird question . . . dozing off . . . English class . . . geometry—geometry! That was it. *I have geometry class then,* Evan had said. She hadn't told him that her English class was first period. How could he have known that it took place at the same time as his geometry class?

"Evan," she began, "how did—"

But just then the timer went off. "Pizza!" said Evan happily. He pulled the pan out of the oven and set it on top of the stove with a flourish. "May I offer you a slice? And a paper towel? We don't have any plates. I don't think we have a knife, either. We're going to have to pull this pizza apart with our bare hands, like cavemen."

In all the finger burning and ouching that followed, Cora forgot what she'd wanted to ask.

"Here are our supersecret, superimportant documents," Evan announced. He and Cora had finished eating; now they were back in the conference room. "Well, not documents, and not secret. Just invitations to the unveiling.

How about if I fold them and you put them in the envelopes?"

"Sounds good."

Cora and Evan had had so few actual conversations that she felt self-conscious at first. But somehow it was easier to talk when her hands were busy. The two of them chatted for an hour without a single awkward pause. At one point Cora heard the footsteps overhead again. "Is that one of the sisters—I mean, one of your bosses?" she asked.

Evan nodded. "They don't get out much. Sometimes they're up all night. They live here, remember."

"Don't they ever come downstairs? To the kitchen, for instance?"

Evan shook his head. "Not all that often, actually. Only when they're in their office down the hall."

"So will we go upstairs when I meet them?"

"*Meet* them?" Evan put down the invitation he was folding. "Why would you want to do that?"

Cora didn't quite know what to answer. "You said they were going to be here, so I guess I assumed I was going to meet them. You work for them—wouldn't they want to know who you're bringing in?"

"Not really. They're busy with other stuff, especially the new statue. They don't have time to get to know anybody. Not right now, at least."

"Yes, but—well, it just seems strange—you'd think they would want to meet another kid who's volunteering for them."

"They wouldn't," said Evan shortly. Head down, he began to fold another invitation.

"But I thought you'd said they'd be 'glad to see fresh blood' or whatever."

"I'm not so sure that'd be best right now."

"Then why did you ask me here? We can always hang out at the pizza parlor or the movies. I don't want you to get in trouble because of me—maybe we should . . ."

Now Evan looked up and met her gaze. "I wanted to see you," he said simply, "and I can't get out of working here. So this was the best thing I could think of."

"Evan, what do you mean? You're a volunteer—you can leave any time you want to!"

But Evan just shook his head. "I can't, but it's too hard to explain." For a second he looked sad, but his face brightened quickly. "Anyway, who wants to talk about work?" he said more cheerfully. "What's your favorite movie?"

In a few minutes they were talking at full speed again. The box of invitations emptied out; the box of stuffed envelopes filled up. At about eight o'clock, they were done.

Evan leaned back and stretched. "It feels good to have that done! Thanks for helping. I would've been here forever without you."

"It was fun," said Cora sincerely. "I almost wish there were more envelopes to fill."

"I have to put up fliers on Monday," said Evan. "I'm supposed to put them up at the high school and middle school, plus around the neighborhood there. Want to give me a hand?"

Cora was about to agree immediately, but something held her back. A strange thought had just floated through her mind: *Careful!* But what could be wrong with hanging out with Evan in broad daylight? "I think I'm free—I'll let you know," she said.

"Someone's picking you up at nine, right? How about a walk in the garden until then?"

"How about a walk *not* in the garden?" asked Cora. "We've been here for a long time. Couldn't we walk around the neighborhood instead?"

"Sure! I'll go grab my backpack."

Alone in the conference room, Cora checked her phone. Nothing major. She remembered that she still hadn't given Evan her number. Would it seem too pushy if she did—too much as if she was pressuring him to call? She'd have to get Hailey's opinion on that.

She stood up to stretch and push aside the blind so she could look out the window. No fog tonight. A brilliant moon was rising over the sculpture garden. In its light the statues looked alert, almost on guard, as if they were watching or waiting for something. With a slight shudder, Cora turned away.

She looked back at the empty doorway impatiently. *Now* what was keeping Evan?

When Cora replayed the last words he'd said to her, she realized that he hadn't mentioned coming back to the conference room. Had he expected her to meet him by the front door once she gathered her things?

She peeked out into the hall. Evan certainly wasn't there. Cora sighed. Which would be worse—waiting forever alone or walking through the dark, gloomy house in search of him? Probably waiting.

As soon as she stepped into the hall, Cora heard a

strange hissing. It wasn't terribly loud, but it sounded menacing somehow.

A fly? No, too loud.

Did a gas leak sound like anything? Cora had no idea. She wasn't even sure what gas leaks were. But she knew they were dangerous. What if Evan had passed out somewhere in this big house?

The doors in the hall were still closed. But at the farthest end Cora could see a crack of light under one of them.

Cora was certain that the hissing was coming from inside that room.

She walked reluctantly down the hall. But when she reached the door, she couldn't make herself knock. Over the hissing, she could hear what sounded like two women. They had weird accents and a strangely formal way of speaking. They had to be the Metaxas sisters.

Cora didn't want to eavesdrop, but she couldn't help overhearing them.

"He must be certain to deliver Andromeda," one of the women said.

"If not, we can merely put him back. Our people are so easy to keep in line."

The first speaker let out an ugly cackle. "True, sister. Which is perhaps why they always remain with us."

Now both women were cackling. At the same time, the hissing was growing louder. Whatever a gas leak was, Cora was pretty sure it wasn't what she was hearing. Besides, she hadn't heard Evan's voice in there. Now that she knew the sisters were on the first floor, did she dare run upstairs?

She took a deep breath to steady herself—and immediately began coughing. Some of the dust that was everywhere must have caught in her throat.

"Who is there?" called one of the women sharply.

Feet were heading heavily toward the other side of the door. Cora turned to run.

But before she had taken more than a couple of steps, a hand from behind clamped hard across her mouth. Someone grabbed her; Cora kicked and twisted, but her assailant was much stronger than she was.

She was being dragged away into the looming darkness of the terrifying old house.

CHAPTER 6

For the second time since Cora had met him, Evan said, "It's just me!" But this time he was talking as quietly as he could. "Don't scream," he murmured. "I had to make sure they didn't run into you." He took his hand off Cora's mouth. "Are you okay?"

"I will be, when you let go of me!"

"Oops. I didn't realize—" Evan still had one arm tight around Cora's waist. Now he let go of her. "The supply closet was the closest place," he said. "Sorry it's so dark."

Cora never imagined that someone could move as fast as Evan, especially when he was pulling her along with him. It wasn't as if she were a giant, but Evan had dragged her around the corner and into this closet so quickly that it had almost seemed like flying. Now they were standing in the dark. The crack under the door supplied only a dim line of light. But Cora's eyes were gradually getting used to the dark, and she could see that Evan had his ear pressed to the closed door.

"I don't hear anything," he whispered. "They must have gone upstairs. Let's get out of here. We'll use the side door."

In a few seconds they were outside, where even the sculpture garden seemed like a relief. When they reached the steps and sat down, there was a long silence. Finally Cora spoke up.

"What was that all about? Why did you tackle and drag me away instead of letting me meet your bosses?"

"You don't understand. This wasn't the right time! They've both been in terrible moods all day," Evan said.

"Evan, are you doing something you shouldn't by having me here? I don't want to get you in trouble."

And I don't want to get myself in trouble either, Cora thought.

"No! No, no! Really, no," Evan said. *"No way,"* he added for emphasis. "Bringing you here is exactly what I should be doing. Because I want to see you as much as I can. It's lonely on the days you're not here, when it's just me and those two—" He gave an exaggerated, cartoony look over his shoulder to make sure the sisters weren't watching them.

Cora started to feel better. Evan really did like her as much as she liked him. And although the evening had been a little weird, it had still been romantic. Here on the front steps, in the dim glow of an overhead lantern, she was sitting next to someone who might be her boyfriend. . . .

But even in this mood, she remembered that strange hissing noise.

"Before you did your Superman thing and dragged me away, I heard this hissing sound from the room where your bosses were working. Do you have any idea what it was?"

"Hissing?" Evan stared at her. "I don't know what you mean. Did it sound like a teakettle? They keep a plug-in kettle in their office."

"This was *nothing* like a teakettle," Cora said.

Evan shrugged. "Must have been the radiator, then. Steam heat hisses a lot, especially in old houses. Just another weird thing about this place, I guess."

Was there anything normal about this place, besides Evan? Cora was almost glad she'd be going home soon. She didn't want to leave Evan, but she was definitely eager to put some distance between herself and the creepy old house.

Cora woke up early on Sunday so that she could get all her homework done before her friends came over. She had promised to tell them about her evening with Evan, and she didn't want any assignments looming over her. It was a good thing she had gotten a head start, because Hailey, Amber, and Skye showed up almost an hour early.

"How did it go?" the three girls chorused before she'd even let them into the house.

"And hi to you too!" said Cora. "It was fine, but I wasn't expecting you yet. Did I get the time wrong?"

"No," said Hailey, unconcerned. "We just couldn't wait one more second."

"Well, you're going to have to wait for a couple of seconds," said Cora as the girls tramped into the house. "I have one more page of Spanish homework."

"Homework!" wailed Amber. "You can't do your homework when you have headline news!"

"Besides, it will make us feel bad for not having started ours," put in Skye.

But Cora was firm. "I'm not going to forget about school just because I have a—" She stopped. Evan wasn't exactly her boyfriend—not yet, anyway. "I'm going to get my Spanish done," she hurried on, "and then I'll tell you *everything*."

"And that's everything," she finished, filling in the girls half an hour later. "Basically we stuffed envelopes and had pizza. And talked a ton." She had decided not to mention the hissing-and-closet adventure. It was too bizarre to explain, and besides, she didn't want the girls thinking Evan was some kind of weirdo.

"It's all about *how* you stuffed the envelopes," said Skye. "It could be businesslike." She squared her shoulders and spoke in the gruffest voice she could manage. "'Ms. Nicolaides, I need these to be ready by nine p.m.'— like that. Or did he give you big meaningful looks while he was folding the invitations?"

Cora couldn't help laughing. "No, but he did pass me some paper towels very romantically."

"Evan wouldn't talk about how lonely it is without you if he didn't like you," Hailey announced. "If he didn't *really* like you."

"And he said he wants to see you as much as he can!" added Amber. "A boy wouldn't say that if he just wanted to be friends. It would be asking for trouble. So you asked him to the dance, right?"

"Well, not quite. I'm going to, though. . . ."

Amber rolled her eyes. "Cora, don't waste any more time! Just do it! After what happened at lunch last week, everyone in the eighth grade is expecting to see you at the dance with Evan."

"What Cora needs is to rehearse," said Hailey. "Cora, pretend I'm you and you're Evan." She began talking in a high squeal that sounded nothing like Cora's voice. "Evan," she squeaked, "would you like to go to the dance with me?" In her normal voice, she added, "Now you say what you think he'll answer."

Cora thought for a minute. Then she said, "I'm sorry, Cora, but I don't like you in that way. You're much too young for me. I like how you help me in the garden, but you're more like a little sister to me than a girlfriend."

Hailey looked despairingly at Amber and Skye. "We have a lot of work to do," she said.

The high school and middle school had been built near a cluster of stores and small businesses. A couple of coffee shops and diners were also close by, as well as a dance studio and a branch of the library. "It's lucky I brought lots of fliers," Evan said to Cora on Monday afternoon. "You can't take a step in this neighborhood without tripping over a public bulletin board. I'm going to hit a few more spots tonight. But I'll need more fliers. Want to swing by the sculpture garden with me?"

Cora groaned. "We've just been walking for an hour and a half! Sure, I'll go, but only if we can get a snack first. I'd bet the deli will be very excited to see us twice in one afternoon."

When they'd provisioned themselves with cans of lemonade and some chips, they set out for the sculpture garden. With each step, Cora became more and more nervous. Not about the garden this time, but about the dance. She had promised her friends that she'd ask

Evan that afternoon, and unfortunately time was running out.

"You're awfully quiet all of a sudden," Evan said. "Is this hike too strenuous?"

"It's not that. It's—I'm sure you'll say no, but would you maybe want to go to the eighth-grade dance with me?" Cora blurted out.

Right away she wanted to slap herself. All that rehearsing with her friends the day before! All the careful, strategic openers they had planned! And *this* was what she'd come up with?

But Evan was smiling broadly. "I thought you'd never ask," he said.

Cora stopped midstep. "What?"

"Well, I had to put up fliers in the middle school," Evan reminded her. "I saw all these posters for the dance. I figured you'd be going, and I kept wondering when you were going to mention it. Then I started wondering *if* you were going to mention it. And then . . . well, I figured you weren't going to mention it. But I hoped I was wrong."

"You were!" said Cora fervently. "I mean, you were right that I wasn't going to mention it. But only because it never would have occurred to me that you would even *think* about going with me."

"I would love to go," Evan told her. He took her hand, and they started walking again. "I had already decided that if you didn't ask me, I'd have to ask *you*. Which would have been weird because it's not my school's dance, so I'm glad it worked out this way."

"Me too," said Cora. Suddenly it was as though the sky opened up—the trees lining the street were greener, the sun was shining brighter than ever, and Cora finally, *finally* had a date to the dance. She couldn't help thinking, *It's so, so lucky that I bought that dress!*

"And here we are," Evan announced fifteen minutes later as they walked up to the sculpture garden. "Do you want to come in with me?"

"Definitely," said Cora. "I don't like being alone here."

"*That's* a little dramatic. Just wait one second while I make sure the bosses aren't downstairs."

As Cora watched, Evan sprinted through the foyer, down the long hallway, and back again. "It's fine," he panted. "No one's here."

Just let it go, Cora told herself. This had been a perfect afternoon. There was no reason to spoil it by wondering why Evan wouldn't want the sisters to meet her.

"I'm going to work on seeing the good points about this place," she said as they headed to the conference room. "It's . . . interesting. There aren't a lot of girls who get to hang around with monsters, even if the monsters are just made of stone."

"I'm hoping you'll get to spend even more time here," Evan said. "Now, where are those fliers? This place has gotten a little disorganized, if you haven't noticed."

Cora pointed. "Aren't they under that vase?"

But that was a pile of press releases. After a few minutes' hunting, they finally found the fliers in a cardboard box marked WINTER SUPPLIES.

"Typical," said Evan. "After you, mademoiselle," he added gallantly.

Cora turned to face him. "There are a couple of things we should figure out about the dance," she said, walking backward out of the doorway. "Do you want to go with my friends and their dates? Or maybe you could have dinner at my house and then we could—"

"Cora! Don't move!" Evan shouted.

But Cora pivoted instinctively. What was it that Evan was looking at with such horror?

The Minotaur.

Its massive human hands were reaching for Cora. Its hideous bull head was lowered, ready to charge.

And it was only inches away.

CHAPTER 7

Just seconds after Cora let loose a bloodcurdling scream, she heard voices and footsteps coming from the other side of the foyer.

"What is this dreadful racket?"

Two women, perhaps just younger than her grandmother, rushed through the front door and across the foyer. When they reached the Minotaur statue, the woman in front maneuvered her way around it and yanked Cora toward her. "Stop these hysterics!" she snapped. "Why are you making so much noise?"

Still shocked, Cora pointed a shaky hand at the statue and gasped out, "H-how did it get here?"

"The Minotaur?" asked the woman, as if there had

been room for Cora to point at anything else. "We have been arranging the statues to prepare for the unveiling of our new arrival. We thought it best to move the Minotaur out of the labyrinth while the hedges were being clipped. I cannot think why the movers chose to bring it inside." From the woman's grim expression, the movers were in trouble.

"But this isn't the Minotaur from the labyrinth!" Cora blurted. "I've seen the one in the labyrinth. He's sitting on a throne."

"Nonsense," said the woman who hadn't yet spoken. "This place belongs to us. There is no seated Minotaur anywhere."

Cora had already guessed that these women had to be Evan's bosses, the Metaxas sisters. For one thing, she had recognized their voices right away, and besides, they were obviously sisters. They looked almost identical, though the woman who had been first to reach Cora was perhaps two or three years older than the other. Both were wearing dull-colored, unstylish clothes. Both also had matching—and ugly—old-fashioned hairstyles in the same dull-reddish gray. For a second Cora wondered if they were wearing wigs.

All right, so they live here and this place belongs to them, Cora told herself stubbornly. *I still know what I saw in the labyrinth, and so does Evan. . . .*

Cora looked around to see Evan awkwardly hanging back by the conference room door near the foyer. "Evan, the Minotaur we saw was sitting down. Right?"

Evan grimaced uncomfortably. "Uh, no. He was charging, actually."

"No way! I may have been wrong about that other statue turning her head, but there's no way I would remember a sitting Minotaur instead of this one."

"We own only one Minotaur," said the second woman.

"And it has always been posed this way," said the first.

They should know, Cora told herself. *It's their museum.* But the conversation was already moving on.

"Evan, I assume this girl is the friend you spoke of," said the first woman.

"Yes, this is Cora," said Evan. Somewhat stiffly, he added, "Cora, these are the women I work for—Eunice and Stesha Metaxas."

Cora extended a reluctant hand, but Eunice just stared at her without moving. Her face hot, Cora dropped her hand. "I'm glad to meet you, Miss Metaxas and Miss—uh—"

"Our first names will be easier," said Stesha. "You need not use 'Miss.'"

"Thank you. Evan's—um—told me so much about you that I feel as if I know you already." *And I see that he wasn't exaggerating,* she thought. "I'm sorry that I overreacted. My friends all say that I've got too much imagination. But the Minotaur is such an impressive statue, it's no wonder I was startled. Will it be returned to the labyrinth once the hedges are clipped?"

"I regret to say that we have not yet reached a decision as to what spot in the garden it will occupy," said Eunice. "We have so much preparation for the unveiling that many matters are escaping our attention."

Stesha added, somewhat grudgingly, "We are grateful for the help you have given Evan. Is there perhaps a chance that you might help next weekend as well? The unveiling is on Sunday. We could use help on Saturday. Our assistant has left us—"

"*Most* inconsiderate of her," interrupted Eunice.

"And we could use more hands."

"I'd be glad to help on Sunday," Cora said cautiously,

"but Saturday night I—we, Evan and I—are going to a dance at my school."

"You may attend your dance," said Eunice, as if it were up to her. "Perhaps you can come for a few hours on Saturday morning?"

Cora was willing to go along with the Minotaur story, but she wasn't willing to go along with this. "I'm saving Saturday so my friends and I can get ready for the dance together."

Evan's face visibly dropped, and Stesha's voice was cold. "That is our loss."

"I can still come on Sunday, though," she offered.

Both women nodded gravely. "That will work for our plans," Eunice said. "And we still have time to order your uniform."

"Uniform?" faltered Cora. "Just for working one day? Why?"

"It is an *important* day," said Stesha. "People from all over the city will be here for the unveiling. We must look our best."

Eunice patted Cora on the shoulder again. "The uniform is a custom-made tunic. You will look as lovely as any of the statues in our garden." Coming from her, the compliment had an unpleasant—borderline creepy—undertone.

Now Stesha spoke up. "If you have recovered from your fit of nerves, let us go measure your height. There is a tape measure in our office."

"My height?"

"For the tunic, of course. The dressmaker will need to know how long to make it."

"But I can tell you how tall I am. I'm—"

"Girls your age are always growing," interrupted Eunice brusquely. "For such an important day, it is best to be sure."

This was getting to be too much. "Is Evan going to wear a tunic too?" asked Cora a bit maliciously.

"Evan will be suitably attired," Stesha said. "The two of you will look well matched and appropriate for the occasion."

Evan was sitting down now. He had picked up Cora's mythology book and was idly leafing through it. She could see him roll his eyes at the "well matched" comment, but he still didn't say anything.

"Come to our office," Eunice said. "This will not take long."

The Metaxas sisters strode down the hall, Cora trailing unhappily after them.

What should have been easy turned out to involve a lot of fuss. The sisters had to first get the tape measure and then something to write with. Clearing a spot for Cora to stand in was also a big deal. Next came finding a notepad. After what seemed like an hour, the information had been recorded and Cora was free to leave.

Evan jumped to his feet as they returned to the foyer. As he did so, a crumpled piece of paper fluttered to his feet. It looked familiar, but Cora was too flustered to look closely. All she wanted to do was get out of there.

"All set?" asked Evan in a fake-hearty voice.

Cora gave him a tight smile. "I think so. Finally."

"She is perfect," Eunice told him, to Cora's surprise. "You are lucky to have found her."

"I agree," said Evan. And he sounded so sincere that Cora forgave him for getting her into all this.

The next day at lunch Cora and her friends finalized their plans for the day of the dance.

Hailey, who loved running things, had a notebook

and pen ready. "First things first: I think it would be best if we don't have a sleepover on Friday night," she said in a brisk, businesslike voice. NO SLEEPOVER, she wrote in big capital letters.

"Hey, wait," protested Skye. "Why can't we have a sleepover?"

"Because we need to *sleep*," said Hailey sternly. "You've heard of beauty sleep, right? If we had a sleepover, we'd stay up too late. By the time the dance started, we'd look tired and stressed. So I think we should meet the next morning at eight."

This time both Amber and Skye spoke up. "That's like the middle of the night!" said Amber. "Haven't *you* ever heard of beauty sleep?"

"But we have so much to do! We have to give each other mani-pedis and facials and moisturize our legs and help with each other's hair. We should work out, too. We want to be calm, yet energized. "

"I think we'll have plenty of time to get everything done if we meet after lunch. Don't you, Cora?" said Amber.

Cora jumped. "Don't I what?"

Amber rolled her eyes. "Don't you think we should

meet after lunch?" she said with exaggerated patience.

"Sure. Whatever you want."

"Have you been listening to any of this?" asked Hailey.

"I was thinking about our mythology project." Cora had actually been thinking about the Minotaur statue, so she wasn't too far off. "Remind me when it's due?"

Hailey flipped the notebook to a different section. "Next Monday. I haven't started any research for it."

Cora sighed. "I'm all caught up in our other classes. But for some reason I haven't felt like doing anything with mythology."

Skye yanked a book out of her overstuffed backpack and started flipping through it. "Let me find the Perseus and Andromeda story. We should definitely—Hey, look at this!" She held out the open book to the other girls. "Here's a picture of Andromeda. Remind you of anyone?"

The page showed poor Andromeda chained to a rock in the middle of the ocean. Perseus was flying above her, looking worried. Which made sense, because a huge openmouthed sea monster was on the verge of swallowing Andromeda, who also looked worried.

"Her hair looks just like yours, Cora," Skye pointed out. "And her eyes are green like yours too."

Amber bent over the picture. "Actually, she looks a *lot* like you, Cora. That's kind of weird. I never noticed it before."

"Me either," said Cora. "But you're right."

"And you're bringing your own personal Perseus to the dance," teased Hailey.

Skye had stopped paying attention to them and was going through her mythology book again. "Okay, so for our presentation, we're going to have to include the story of how Perseus was raised on that little island. And we'll want to talk about Medusa and her sisters. And—"

"Wait a minute," said Cora. "Medusa had sisters?"

"Uh-huh." Skye flipped through a few pages until she found the Medusa chapter. "Two of them. Euryale and—I don't know how to pronounce it—Sthenno. They were just as horrible-looking as Medusa. You sure don't hear about them as much as Medusa, because it was Medusa who was killed by Perseus. So I guess that would make her more famous."

"I can't believe I missed them!" Cora pulled out her own textbook. "What page are you on?"

"One hundred forty-three."

Quickly Cora leafed through the pages. When she got to the right spot, she paused. Frowning, she turned back a couple of pages. Then she took the book by the spine and gave it a shake.

Nothing fell out.

"Um, Cora? What are you doing?" asked Hailey.

"I'm looking for the right page," Cora said slowly. An unexpected image had just flashed through her mind.

Yesterday afternoon. At the museum. When Evan had stood up, a piece of paper had fallen to the floor. From his lap, maybe? Or from the book he'd been reading—which was Cora's mythology textbook.

She closed her eyes and tried to remember what the piece of paper had looked like. She hadn't been paying much attention at the time. . . .

No, she couldn't remember anything about the way it looked. But here, right in front of her, she could plainly see that the page about Euryale and Sthenno had been torn out.

CHAPTER 8

Cora knew right away that she couldn't share the details about the missing book page with her friends. It would have been impossible to explain. As she thought about it that night in bed, she couldn't even figure out a way to explain it to herself.

If Evan had torn out the page, why would he have done it? She remembered him saying that her mythology book had gotten a few of the details wrong, but would he really go so far as to tear out the bad pages?

If he hadn't done it, then what was the piece of paper she'd seen? And if he hadn't torn out the page, who had? Those textbooks were brand new. Ms. Finch had made a big deal about "respecting" them.

But if he *had* done it—for whatever reason—it meant she was spending all her time with a guy who tore pages out of books and didn't tell her. . . .

Which just couldn't be true. Cora was sure it couldn't. Maybe she didn't know everything about human nature, but she knew she could trust her instincts on this. Something weird might be going on, but Evan himself was trustworthy. And he really liked her. Cora sat up in bed and tried to smooth her rumpled sheets. *If I didn't have such a big imagination, this wouldn't be such a problem,* she thought. *I would know I could trust what I saw. I wouldn't freak out about stuff that can't happen—like statues moving, or Evan looking into my English class.*

But those fantasies had colored everything. However hard she tried, Cora couldn't feel quite the same about Evan as she had. One way or another, there was something . . . unreliable about him.

Cora punched her pillow. She was overthinking this again. It was time to stop obsessing about this! Evan was a great guy. He was taking her to the dance, and they would have a wonderful time.

"There are no problems," Cora said aloud. Except that she'd better start coming up with some ideas for the

Perseus and Andromeda project. She sure wasn't going to have time to do it this coming weekend.

On Saturday morning, Cora sprang out of bed the second she opened her eyes. This was going to be a big day.

Her dress, in its special garment bag, was already draped over her desk chair. Her strappy sandals were in a shoe bag next to the chair. (This might be the one time in its life that the shoe bag—a present from her aunt—would be used.) Makeup bag: check. Hairbrush: check. Earrings and necklace: check.

Breakfast: not check. Cora headed down to the kitchen. She was just pouring herself some milk when her phone rang.

"Cora." It was Evan's voice.

Uh-oh. That didn't sound like a great way to start a conversation, especially so early in the morning.

"Yes?" said Cora cautiously.

"I have some bad news."

Cora winced. *Please, please let this not be about the dance!*

"I have to work tonight."

"*What?* I thought the pizza place had given you the night off!"

Evan's voice was heavy. "They did. But I have to work at the museum all day. There's a lot of last-minute stuff to help get ready for the unveiling tomorrow. I have a ton of errands to run, and the sisters need me at the museum, probably at least until eight o'clock tonight."

"But—but the dance is at seven."

Cora's dad passed by the kitchen just then and gave her a questioning look. Angrily Cora waved him away.

"I know. I won't be done by then."

"Why can't you just say no this *once?*" she wailed at Evan. "You always act as if they own you!"

Evan was silent for a second. Then he said, "I don't think I can make you understand."

Cora would have been willing to argue forever, but Evan sounded so miserable that she couldn't stay mad. Staring at the ceiling, she allowed herself a silent moment to swallow back the tears that were welling up. Then—in a fake, perky voice—she chirped, "Let's figure out a way to make it work."

"You're the best," said Evan. "I mean it. The. Best. I'll make it up to you somehow."

"Why don't you make it up to me now by coming up with an idea?"

"Well, the simplest thing would just be to get there late," Evan said.

"We can't. They're not letting anyone in after seven thirty. Let's see, let's see . . .Why don't I help with your errands? Where do you have to go?"

"Um . . . to the supermarket, for hors d'oeuvres. The bakery, for the cake. I have to refill the postcard piles at the library. And I have to get to the Hitchens Museum to set up a delivery. They're lending us a special bench pedestal for the day." He paused, then added, "Just boring stuff like that."

"It doesn't sound boring! It sounds like fun! And when we're all done with the errands, we can go to the sculpture garden and I can help with whatever you have to do there. I bet we can finish everything up in plenty of time to get to the dance."

"But I hate to ask you to do all this. For one thing, you wouldn't have time to go home and get ready."

Cora had just been thinking about that. "I could get ready at the museum when we're done working. I could bring my dress and my other stuff. We're not going to be doing anything messy like planting trees, are we?"

Evan laughed. "No, no. Just tidying up. Photocopying the programs for tomorrow. Stuff like that."

"Well, then?"

"Well, then, okay!" said Evan. "Do you think one of your parents could pick me up at noon and then drop us off at the supermarket? That would save some time right there."

"Fine. But first I'd better tell my friends that I won't be meeting them at Hailey's to get ready. Wish me luck! They're not going to be happy about it."

Cora's mother wasn't too pleased either. "I wanted to take pictures," she protested, "and now I won't even get to see what you look like before the dance."

"I'm disappointed too," Cora answered. "I wanted everything to be traditional. But this way is better than not going at all."

"How about if I swing by the museum just before you leave for the dance? That way I could at least get a photo of you and Evan."

"Mom! Please, no! Things are complicated enough

already. I don't want you getting all in Evan's face with a camera."

"I won't get all in his face," said Mrs. Nicolaides indignantly. "It's really your picture I care about, anyway."

"Well, you're going to have to use your imagination. Imagine that I'm radiantly beautiful and Evan is stunningly handsome. That will bring you close to the truth."

"Also, what are you going to do about supper?" asked Cora's mother. "Take some sandwiches or something."

"No sandwiches," said Cora firmly. "We're going to the supermarket and a bakery. We can pick something up there. Don't worry! It's all going to be great."

She hoped she was right.

Cora didn't have to hunt for Evan when she got to the garden. He was in the house's foyer, pacing around as he waited for her.

His first words were, "There's a coat closet in the conference room. You can hang your dress in there."

"You could say hi first," Cora teased him.

"Yeah, you're right. Hi. Let's put your stuff in the closet and get out of here."

Cora took a step back to look at him. "Evan, what's the matter? You look all nervous."

"I kind of am," confessed Evan as they headed for the conference room. "So many details, and feeling pulled in so many directions—it feels as if today has too many moving parts. It's nice of your dad to give us a ride, though."

Once they were in the car, Evan seemed to cheer up. "So what did Hailey and everyone say?" he asked.

"You do *not* want to know," Cora said. "Anyway, I got through it. They may even speak to us at the dance if we're very, very nice to them."

"Here's the supermarket," Cora's dad said a few minutes later as he turned into the entrance of the parking lot. "Are you okay from here on?"

"Yup," said Evan and Cora at the same time.

"It's lucky the supermarket delivers," Cora said an hour later. "That was a huge list."

It had actually been fun to grocery shop with Evan. They had roamed the aisles picking out whatever they thought looked partyish. ("This is one thing the sisters totally wouldn't be able to do," Evan said. "The only party food they know about is olives.") When Evan had paid and arranged for the delivery, he and Cora headed to the bakery, which was a short walk away.

"Do we get to pick out a bunch of stuff here, too?" asked Cora.

"Unfortunately, no. We get to pick out a cake. And it has to be something Eunice and Stesha will like. That means not too sweet and not too decorated."

Cora made a face. "Boring, in other words. Or with a gross filling, like figs."

Evan opened the door to the bakery, and they both headed inside.

"We need to order a cake," Evan told the baker's assistant.

The assistant, a young woman, looked confused. "For the two of you?"

"No, no. It needs to serve a lot of people. It's for an art opening."

"Cool! Is there a picture you want us to copy?" asked the woman. "We can airbrush anything you want onto cakes. How about the *Mona Lisa*?"

It took a while to convince her that they weren't

interested in a *Mona Lisa* cake. Evan also had to talk her out of her next idea—a statue-shaped cake with gray icing. Finally they settled on a dark-chocolate sheet cake with a bitter, dark-chocolate icing.

"Is there any sugar in this at all?" Cora asked, wrinkling her nose.

"This icing has a sophisticated flavor," the assistant said kindly. "Really more of an adult thing."

"Just right for Eunice and Stesha," said Evan. "They disapprove of desserts."

Cora was still trying to get the bitter taste out of her mouth. "They should approve of this then," she said. "It punishes you with every bite."

After the bakery came the postcard drop-off at the library and a short stop for lunch. Then Evan and Cora stuck up a few last-minute flyers. Finally they boarded a bus that would take them across town to the Hitchens Museum.

"Why did we have to come this far to borrow a pedestal?" asked Cora as they climbed down the steps of the bus.

Evan shrugged. "Eunice and Stesha know the owner. Some of their sculptures are actually here on loan for an exhibit. We can see them if you want."

Cora was half-inclined to say that she'd already seen enough of the Metaxas statues and didn't need any reminders. But when Evan had arranged for the loan of the pedestal, and the two of them were on their way out, they actually passed the exhibit Evan had mentioned.

"Look!" Evan stopped at the entrance to the room and pointed at one display case. "Let's take a quick look."

Cora sighed loudly. "All right. One minute, but then we *really* have to go."

"I recognize that hedgehog," Evan said as they approached a cluster of cute little animal statues.

"Oh, it's not the huge garden sculptures!" said a relieved Cora.

"No, this is just animals and plants and vases. Small stuff." He gestured toward a plaque on the wall that read FLORA AND FAUNA OF THE CLASSICAL ERA.

Cora grinned. "As long as there are no Minotaurs, it's fine by me."

It was the kind of exhibit Cora especially liked. Not big grand "educational" objects, but glimpses of everyday life in the past. Three rooms were filled with pottery, jewelry, and paintings featuring animals or plants in some way. Somehow it surprised Cora whenever she realized that artists from centuries before had been interested in animals and plants just the way she was.

"It's amazing, isn't it?" asked Evan. "These statues are two thousand years old, and there's still so much detail you can see in them."

"You're right," agreed Cora. She was looking at a tiny kitten sculpture, carved from black obsidian. "Look, a kitten! Why can't they have some cute sculptures on display at the garden?"

"I don't know—you have to admit, it's cute, but it's not the most impressive thing in the world," Evan said.

"I guess so," Cora said, turning to Evan. "But this kitten definitely makes me happier—"

She had just turned to look at the obsidian kitten again. Before, the kitten had been standing upright. Now it was arching its back.

Cora gasped. "Evan! Did you see that?"

"Did I see what?"

"It's not the same statue! The kitten wasn't arched that way."

Evan's face was blank. "Uh, no," he said slowly after a second. "It was arched. Are you okay?"

"Of course I am!" snapped Cora, glaring at him. "I'm not seeing things. It was definitely—"

In the instant she'd glanced away, the statue had changed position again. Now the kitten had fangs bared, poised to spring straight at her.

Without thinking, Cora jumped back.

"Careful! Wait! *Stop!*" yelled Evan. "There's a pedestal there—"

His warning came too late. Cora had already backed into the pedestal. There was a terrible crash behind her as a glass display case toppled to the floor and shattered.

"Oh no!" gasped Cora. "What did I do?"

"Miss! Step away from there!" A guard was running up to her, another guard right behind him.

"Don't walk on any glass," said Evan. He took Cora's arm and guided her a few feet to the side.

Horrified, Cora stared down at the floor. Broken glass was everywhere. In the middle of the jagged shards were the remains of an ancient vase, cracked into eight or ten pieces.

"What was that?" she half whispered.

Evan, she saw, was looking a little pale. He pointed at the display card.

"'Greek wine amphora,'" Cora read aloud. "From 150 BCE. Torpedo-shaped clay vessel showing the struggle between Herakles and Apollo. On loan from the'—" She stopped, and Evan finished reading for her.

"'On loan from the Metaxas Sculpture Garden.'"

CHAPTER 9

"Miss, you are in serious trouble," snapped the first guard. The guard behind him was already muttering into his walkie-talkie.

"You don't have to tell me that," moaned Cora. "Was it valuable?"

"Probably," said Evan. "But don't worry," he added, not very convincingly.

"Don't *worry*? Will I have to go to jail?"

"Of course not. You didn't—"

"You're both going to need to come with me," interrupted the first guard.

"Wait," said Evan. "I work for the museum that the vase belonged to. I should call the owners right away."

At the guard's nod, Evan pulled out his phone and quickly punched in the number.

"Eunice?" he said after a second. "Oh, Stesha. Hello. Um, we're at the Hitchens, and there's a problem."

Cora couldn't bear to look at Evan as he told Stesha what had happened. She stared at the ceiling, trying not to cry.

"Yes, there's a guard right here," she heard Evan say. "Two of them. Do you want to—okay."

He held the phone out to the first guard. "I have one of the owners right here. She'd like to talk to you."

The guard listened without expression, then handed the phone back to Evan. "They'll be here in ten minutes, she says. And she wants you two to wait here with me."

"Can we at least sit down?" asked Evan.

"Sure. Use that bench over there."

It was the worst—and longest—ten minutes Cora had ever lived through. Evan didn't say a word, and she couldn't bring herself to break the silence. The first guard stood in the doorway, his eyes fixed on them as if they might try to escape. The second had disappeared, perhaps to make a report.

There goes the dance, Cora thought wretchedly. Whatever

happened, she was sure Evan wouldn't want to go now. And the vase had to have been valuable—was she going to have to pay for it? She had a feeling that extra babysitting wouldn't cover it. What would the cost do to her parents? Would they go broke paying the sisters back?

Evan wouldn't want to see her anymore—she was sure of that. Oh, if only she hadn't suggested helping him today! She hadn't helped him a bit. She had only—

"Here they are," Evan said in an undertone as Eunice and Stesha swept into the room. He jumped to his feet and walked over to them, Cora following uncertainly behind him.

"Show us," said Eunice imperiously, before anyone else could say a word.

They led her and Stesha to the pile of broken glass and pottery. In silence, the two women bent over to look at the damage. Almost immediately they both stood up again.

"Pah! It is nothing," said Eunice.

"What do you mean?" asked Cora. "It was thousands of years old!"

"Correct, but it was not particularly rare. Or interesting."

"In any case, this type of vase is easy to come by and will be easily repaired," put in Stesha. "The important thing, Cora, is that *you* were not hurt."

"Just so," agreed Eunice. "Compared to you, the vase is meaningless. *You* are the real treasure."

"I—what? I am?"

"Indeed," said Stesha. "We are lucky to have met you. And so is Evan."

Cora thought that sounded a little over the top, but it was better than having the sisters angry at her.

She turned to Evan. "We don't have to go to the dance," Cora said. "Really, I feel like I should make it up to you all by working tonight."

"Nonsense," said Stesha. "Tonight is your big night. If you would like, you may help us with the few remaining chores at the garden, but then you should go to your dance."

"Really?" said Cora, on the verge of tears.

"Really," Eunice echoed. "Put this from your mind. It was only an accident."

"Oh thank you so much!" Cora said. Evan took her hand and looked down at her. There was a sadness in his eyes she didn't understand, but there wasn't any time to linger on what had happened—the dance was just three hours away!

"Here we are," Eunice said as the four of them pulled up to the sculpture garden. Cora was happy that things had worked out and was ready to tackle the list of chores that were left for the unveiling tomorrow.

As she and Evan reviewed the list, Cora thought the different tasks seemed refreshingly ordinary compared to what she'd just been through. Besides, every task they could cross off brought them closer to the dance!

As the sisters headed back to their office, Evan turned to her. "Do you want to work together, or should we divide and conquer?"

"We might as well split up," Cora answered. "You can do all the heavy lifting, but we have to keep track of the time."

For the next couple of hours the two of them worked at top speed. Cora had to photocopy a bunch of programs for the next day's event. (The photocopier had a temper tantrum at first, but finally she calmed it down.) She washed way too many dishes. (Hadn't the sisters ever heard of cleaning up as they went along?) She even had to iron some backdrops for a couple of displays in the little museum. (Which basically meant learning how to use an iron.) She also checked the time about once a minute, which was a job in itself. Before she knew it, everything on her part of the list was done.

Cora sighed with satisfaction as she put away the last of the clean dishes. True, this hadn't been the prepare-for-the-dance day she'd been counting on. But everything had worked out after all. She was pretty sure she would take longer to get ready than Evan, so why not get started now? She practically skipped down the hall to the conference room. Eagerly she pulled open the closet door.

Her shoes and makeup bag were right where she'd left them.

But the clothes rack was empty. Her dress for the dance was gone.

For what felt like the millionth time since she'd first visited the Metaxas Sculpture Garden, Cora couldn't believe her eyes. She scanned the conference room. Could the dress have slipped off its hanger and fallen somewhere? But the closet floor was bare.

Don't panic, Cora told herself. *Dresses don't get lost.*

Maybe someone had moved it? But why would anyone do that?

Evan might know. If he didn't, he would help Cora search. She ran outside to find him.

The weather was starting to change. It was colder, and the sky was clouding up. A stiff breeze was blowing too. Even while Cora headed for the maintenance shed, her brain was ticking through dance details.

We can't walk to the dance if it starts to rain. I'll have to call Mom for a ride. I hope she and Dad haven't gone out to dinner or something.

Her mother could even bring her camera and take a few pictures for the scrapbook! That would make her happy.

Now she had reached the maintenance shed—which was locked. And unless he had somehow trapped himself inside the shed, Evan wasn't there.

Was that his voice calling her, or just the wind? Someone was whispering her name.

"Cora! Help me!"

"Where are you?" Cora yelled back.

"Over here! Come quick!"

"Okay, but where?"

"Here . . ."

The voice trailed off and was lost in a strong gust of wind.

Was it Evan? What had happened to him? Cora rushed toward the spot where she thought she'd heard the voice. Leaves and twigs were starting to blow around now. She could feel them hitting her ankles.

Can't walk to the dance in this crazy weather . . .

She'd gone perhaps thirty feet when someone grabbed her by the hair.

Cora shrieked as she skidded to a stop. For an instant the shock and pain were blinding. Then her vision cleared, and she saw that it wasn't a human hand that had grabbed her but a statue's stone one. Her hair was knotted in the fingers of one of the centaurs.

She heard herself yelling "Stop it! Let me go!" Frantically she tried to untangle the snarls, but the wind kept winding her hair farther and farther within the centaur's grasp—or was it the centaur's hand that was moving?

"Evan, help!" she wailed. Her head was held at such an awkward angle that her voice sounded thin and tiny. Then, suddenly, Evan was at her side.

"Wow," he said.

"Don't stand there making comments—help me!"

"Wow," Evan repeated. Then, "Sorry. It's just that you're . . . really tangled up. I don't know where to start."

"Start anywhere," begged Cora. "I can't reach."

"Okay, okay." He sounded a little frantic. "Here, let's start with the thumb. Not your thumb—the statue's. This is some kind of centaur holding you, by the way."

"He's doing a good job," Cora said.

"Does this hurt?" Carefully Evan lifted a section of hair free.

"Kind of, but—hey! Where were you, speaking of getting hurt? What was the matter?"

"Huh? What do you mean?"

"You were calling out to me, weren't you?"

"I wasn't—maybe you thought you heard something in the wind? What are *you* doing outside, anyway? Shouldn't you be getting ready?"

"Yes, I definitely should. Only my dress isn't in the conference room."

"What?" Evan stopped a second to stare at her. "Where is it?"

"That's what I want to know. I checked the closet,

and then I came out to ask if you had seen it anywhere."

"Only in the conference room when you hung it there," said Evan as he went back to untangling her. "You closed the door when we went out, right?"

Cora's heart lurched. "I'm . . . not sure. I think so. But no one would take a *dress*. My other stuff is all where I left it."

"It probably got moved somewhere." Evan tried to soothe her as he freed the last of her hair from the centaur's hand. "We'll find it."

They didn't.

Together, Cora and Evan searched the first floor: the foyer, the conference room, the museum rooms, and even the broom closet. The only place they couldn't get into was the sisters' office, which was locked.

"The sisters know we're going to the dance," said Evan. "They would never have moved your dress in the first place, much less locked it in their office."

Cora knew he was right, but it didn't stop her from wanting to check the office anyway. "Don't you have a key?" she asked.

Evan shook his head. "This is the one room I can't open."

Cora wanted to scream, she was so frustrated. "It's almost time to leave! What am I going to do?" she wailed.

"Why not wear your tunic?" suggested Evan.

"My tu—what are you talking about?"

"You know," said Evan. He sounded maddeningly calm. "The uniform you'll be wearing tomorrow. No one will guess that it's a uniform."

"I am *not* wearing a *tunic* to a school dance," said Cora through clenched teeth.

"Why not? It's really pretty."

"But—" Cora broke off and sighed. "Okay, I'll take a look. Where is it?"

"It's upstairs. I'll run and get it."

A minute later Evan came back carrying a flat, white cardboard box. He set it down on the conference table and, with a flourish, lifted off the top.

Cora stared down in silence. It wasn't as bad as she'd feared. At least this dress looked nothing like a uniform. The tunic was white, with a braided golden belt and straps made of the same braided material. The fabric was pleated silk, or something like silk, and it fell to just above her knee.

"It's not something I would buy," she said with a sigh, "but it's not terrible. Anyway, I guess I don't have a choice."

"I'll go get ready upstairs," said Evan. He gave her shoulder a comforting squeeze. "Don't worry. We'll have a great time no matter what you're wearing."

Cora closed the conference room door behind him. There was no mirror here, but that didn't matter. She didn't even want to see herself in the tunic. She'd been planning to give herself a pedicure, but she now didn't care enough to bother. She'd also hoped to put her hair into an updo, but an updo combined with a tunic would look like a costume.

Time to get this show on the road. . . .

Forlornly she shrugged herself into the tunic. She slipped on her shoes and put on the bracelet and earrings she had brought. For just a minute she wondered if it was too late to get out of going to the dance at all. Then she squared her shoulders, opened the door, and walked into the hall.

Evan was out there waiting for her. He was wearing a T-shirt and jeans. He looked great—and normal. To Cora's surprise, his face lit up when he saw her.

"You look perfect. *Perfect*. Like a Greek goddess."

"Indeed she does," came a harsh voice from down the hall.

Startled, Cora turned to see Eunice and Stesha standing outside their office. Where had they come from?

"We have been putting things in order for tomorrow," said Stesha, as if she could read Cora's thoughts.

"Everything must be in order," added Eunice oddly.

Stesha's eyes looked brighter than Cora had ever seen them. Maybe it was a trick of the light, but they seemed *too* bright. They weren't shining; they were glowing. Cora glanced at Eunice and saw that her eyes too, looked oddly bright.

"It is a pleasure to see you in your tunic," said Eunice. "We chose exactly right." She gave a hollow chuckle. "And so did Evan."

"Thanks," said Evan after an awkward pause. "Well, Cora, shall we get going? I think we can beat the rain."

"All the doors are locked but one," Stesha told him. "You must leave through the side door that opens onto the garden."

It was starting to dawn on Cora that what she was feeling wasn't excitement. It was dread. She didn't want to go to the dance. Not just because of what she was wearing, but because of the whole setup. The broken vase, her lost dress, the Metaxas sisters' strange eyes, the crazy wind . . . everything seemed wrong, somehow.

"We should get going," she said nervously. "We don't want to be late."

"No indeed," said Eunice. "Go with Evan. This is your big night."

"Absolutely," chimed in Stesha. She moved forward a couple of steps to stand next to her sister. "Your big night. *Very* big."

Standing motionless, shoulder to shoulder—their expressions identical, their eyes burning—the sisters looked like a dreadful illustration in an old book. Suddenly Cora couldn't stand to be near them any longer. She turned and rushed for the side door with Evan at her side.

From behind her, Stesha spoke again. "A *very* big night," she repeated. "And now it begins."

CHAPTER 10

"This way," said Evan as he grabbed Cora's hand and began pulling her across the lawn.

"But the gate's over there!" Cora pointed in the opposite direction.

"It's okay. I know a shortcut," Evan told her. "We should hurry—I think it's going to rain any minute."

The sky did look ominous, and the air felt heavy and humid. It was so windy that Cora was glad she hadn't tried to put her hair up. Her strappy sandals kept gouging into the grass, making it hard to keep up with Evan's long strides. Worse, the tunic snagged on every statue they passed.

"The statues feel as if they're closing in on us," she

panted. "My dress will be shredded by the time we get to school."

"Be careful in the labyrinth, then," said Evan. "Don't let the dress get caught on the branches."

"The *labyrinth*? Why are we going into the labyrinth?"

"That's how we get to the shortcut," Evan said, walking even faster.

Cora tried to stop, but he wouldn't let her. "Evan, what do you mean? You're not making any sense!"

But Evan wouldn't turn to look at her. They were at the entrance to the labyrinth now. Without answering, he pulled her into the maze.

"You're hurting my wrist! Let me go!"

"The center is the only way out," Evan said.

The grim determination in his voice scared Cora more than anything else that had happened that night. They were half running now as Evan made his way along the paths. Once Cora tripped and twisted her ankle, but Evan only yanked her to her feet and kept going.

After too many turns to keep track of, they reached the center of the maze. The Minotaur on his throne had been replaced by a stone bench.

"Here we are," said Evan. He guided Cora to the

bench, and she sat down hesitantly. He sat beside her.

"This is where they're going to put the Andromeda statue," he said sadly. "Right in the center, where she can never get out." Evan's voice was indescribably sad.

"Okay," Cora said, "but why are *we* here?"

Evan sighed. "I kept telling you it was too hard to explain. Remember when you told me that the sisters don't own me?"

"Y-yes."

"Well, in a way they do. They'll only let me go if I do them a favor. Just this one favor."

"Let you go?" echoed Cora. How could this conversation be real? Was she dreaming again? "What kind of favor?"

He didn't seem to have heard the question. "Believe me, I hate having to do this. *Hate* it. If there were another way, *any other way*, I would have—I would have—" He took her hands in one of his. With his other hand he gently brushed a loose strand of hair off her face. "At least you won't feel anything," he said in a broken voice.

Before Cora could answer, a strange hissing sound interrupted them.

"What's that?" And where had Cora heard it before?

A trampling of branches underfoot. The rustling of leaves. Someone was coming, and the hissing was getting louder.

Suddenly Cora remembered where she'd heard that hissing before. It had been coming from behind the closed door of the Metaxas sisters' office that day. Now it was coming closer and closer to the center of the labyrinth.

"What's happening? Who's coming?" Cora's voice was sharp with fear.

"I'm so sorry" was all Evan said. "The statues—when the stars are aligned, some of them can move, just a little. They were trying to warn you. They were doing what they knew I couldn't."

"Warn me about what? Evan, you're scaring me!"

Louder hissing now.

Evan turned toward the sound. He squeezed Cora's hand and took a deep breath.

Then, suddenly, he jumped to his feet. "I can't do this," he said. "I *won't* do this. Not to you. *No!*" he shouted. "Wait! I've changed my mind! I'll stay! Just let her go!"

He yanked Cora to her feet. "Run, Cora! *Run!* You've got to get out of here. Go through the—"

Suddenly his face changed. *"No,"* he called again to someone behind Cora. "You can't do this to her! Take me!"

Cora turned to look. Standing behind her, shoulder to shoulder, were Eunice and Stesha. But something was terribly different about them.

As she watched, the sisters reached up and pulled off their hair. No—their wigs, of course. The wigs Cora had noticed the first time she met them.

Now Cora saw clearly the nest of red snakes hissing and writhing where their hair should have been. With sickening horror she realized that the snakes were growing out of their skulls.

Snakes instead of hair . . .

"Medusa had two sisters," Cora gasped.

"Correct," said Euryale. There was a dreadful, gloating smile on her face. "The forgotten sisters, Euryale and Sthenno. And this is our Perseus, of course. To think that we almost lost him."

"You were so foolish, Perseus," said Sthenno. "Why did you not leave the girl and claim your reward? You could have tasted sweet freedom for the first time in—how long has it been? Two hundred years? Three hundred?" The snakes swirled sickeningly as she shook her head. "Instead you wait here and we get you both. Foolish, foolish mortals."

It was all becoming clear to Cora. The empty Perseus pedestal they'd seen in the sculpture garden. The other statues, so disturbingly lifelike, trying to warn her away. The torn-out page from her mythology book. Her missing dress . . . the tunic she was wearing now . . .

Evan had been the Perseus statue.

He had told her that he needed to do one last favor for the sisters, and now Cora realized what the favor was. To win his freedom, Evan had brought her here, just in time for her school dance, when she'd be dressed up to look as lovely as any of the statues in their garden.

Medusa's sisters would turn her into stone. *She* was going to be the new Andromeda statue.

Cora tried to move but found that she couldn't. She couldn't even speak. She looked at Evan.

Only his blank, gray, stone eyes met hers.

EPILOGUE

"I still don't understand any of this," said Hailey. "I know Cora likes this place, but to skip the dance last night?"

"Without talking to one of us," added Amber. "That is totally not like Cora."

"I guess she was having a great time here," said Skye. "She and Evan must have been having so much fun that they decided not to leave. I don't see Evan anywhere either."

It was the morning after the eighth-grade dance. Last night's rain had cleared the air. Today was bright and sunny—perfect for the unveiling of the new statue at the Metaxas Sculpture Garden. A lot of people must have thought the same thing; the garden's labyrinth was packed with visitors. Cora's friends were on the edge of the crowd, trying to spot her, but it was hard to see anything besides the backs of the adults in front of them.

"Another thing I don't understand," said Hailey, "is why anyone thinks these statues are worth seeing." She gave a little shudder. "They all look sad, or scared, or both. How could Cora stand working here?"

"Cora's interested in lots of things," said Skye loyally. "Plus, she wanted to be with Evan. Maybe he couldn't get away."

Hailey was frowning. "She could still have—"

A woman's voice broke in. "Welcome, friends!"

The woman was standing on a small dais so she could be seen. In front of the dais was something draped in a cloth. Next to her stood—

"Are they twins?" whispered Hailey.

"They sure look the same amount of weird," Amber whispered back. "I can't believe Cora is missing this!"

The two women were dressed in identical gray frocks with capes of a darker gray. Not the kind of thing you'd expect anyone to wear for a festive occasion. But what the girls noticed—what they couldn't help noticing— were the women's matching hairstyles.

"Are those wigs?" said Skye in her normal voice. A man in front of her turned and glared at the girls. "They *look* like wigs," Skye murmured.

"I am Eunice Metaxas, and this is my sister, Stesha," the first woman was saying. She had a heavy accent. "Today is an occasion we have long awaited.

"Our Perseus statue, as some of you know, has been quite lonely without a companion—the lovely Andromeda. If you are familiar with Greek mythology, you will know that Perseus was the young man who murdered Medusa."

"'Murdered?'" repeated Hailey.

"For this deed, Perseus was not punished by the gods," Eunice continued. "Instead, they applauded him. And, as he returned home, carrying the head of his victim, Perseus saw a lovely young woman chained to a rock. This was Andromeda. Perseus rescued her, and the rest is history—at least to the Greeks."

There was a sprinkling of polite laughter from the crowd.

Now Stesha took up the story. "The Metaxas Sculpture Garden contains a Perseus statue of remarkable quality," she said. "A similarly lifelike Andromeda has been difficult to find, but at last we have succeeded."

She gestured toward the cloth-covered object in front of her. "I present to you—Andromeda. With her Perseus, together at last."

Someone whisked the cloth away. Now the applause was loud and enthusiastic. "Amazing," said the man who had frowned at the girls.

"I can't see!" said Skye.

"Me neither," said Hailey. She was standing on tiptoe and craning her neck. "We'll just have to wait to get up there."

Even the most remarkable statue can be looked at only so long. After a minute or two the crowd in front of the girls began to melt away so that they could move forward.

When they reached the spot where the statues were standing, all three girls gasped.

The Andromeda statue was seated. The one of Perseus hovered over it protectively. Like so many of the other statues, the stone figures bore identical looks of horror.

They were perfect replicas of Cora and Evan.

Hailey broke a long silence. "No way."

Skye sounded troubled. "It's not that they're *like* Cora and Evan. It's that they're exactly like them. *Exactly*," she said again. "Did Cora and Evan model for these?"

"Both statues are ancient," came Eunice's voice behind her. Startled, the girls turned to see that the two Metaxas sisters had come up right behind them.

"Many centuries old," Eunice continued. "Yet there can be no doubt that they were created by the same artist."

"There sure can't." Amber was staring at the statue that looked like Cora. "They look so real! In fact, they look like people we actually know," she added.

"Many Greeks have the same facial features," said Stesha. "Perhaps your friends are of Greek ancestry?"

"Our friend Cora is," Hailey told her.

"Many sculptors rely on facial templates for inspiration. Your friend's Greek heritage combined with a similar facial template might explain the likeness."

"I—I guess so," Hailey said after a second. But she sounded as if it hadn't explained anything. "Cora looks exactly like the Andromeda statue. Or the Andromeda statue looks exactly like Cora. Or something."

"Anyway, I wish Cora were here to see this," Skye said, sighing.

The crowd was thinning out now. As Amber and Skye took a few steps toward the labyrinth's exit, Hailey ventured one last glance at the Andromeda statue. "Hey, guys," Hailey called, turning to the other girls. "Wasn't the statue's mouth closed a few minutes—"

Behind her, Hailey felt a rough stone hand brush against her own—the Andromeda statue was reaching for her.

Hailey jerked her hand away in horror and ran after her friends to the exit.

TURN THE PAGE FOR A
SNEAK PEEK AT

You're invited to a

CREEPOVER®

Truth or Dare

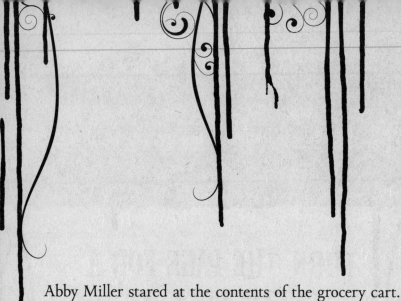

Abby Miller stared at the contents of the grocery cart. "Okay, we've got soda, we've got veggies and dip, we've got popcorn," she said. "Do we need anything else?"

"What about chips?" Leah Rosen, Abby's best friend, asked.

Abby nodded. "You go get some chips and I'll find something good for breakfast."

Leah disappeared around the corner, leaving the cart behind for Abby. Abby wandered through the store to the frozen food section and stood in front of the breakfast case, weighing the waffle options: plain or buttermilk or blueberry or apple cinnamon or—

Suddenly Abby had the creepiest feeling that she was being watched. In the chrome edges of the case, she thought she saw something move.

But when she glanced behind her, no one was there. She was the only person in the frozen food aisle.

Abby turned back to the freezer case and opened the glass door. She was reaching for a box of buttermilk waffles when—

"BOO!"

Abby shrieked as she felt a swift tug on her hair. She spun around to see Leah grinning at her.

"Gotcha!" Leah exclaimed. "Wow, I really spooked you, huh? You have goose bumps!"

"Yeah, from the freezer." Abby laughed, gesturing to the frosty air pouring out of the open case.

"Sure, Ab. Whatever you say," Leah replied, her eyes twinkling. "Check out what I got!"

Abby wrinkled her nose. "Barbecue chips? You know I don't like barbecue!"

"More for me," Leah said with a grin. "Don't worry, you're covered." She tossed a bag of tortilla chips into the cart and placed a jar of salsa next to it.

Abby added two boxes of frozen waffles. "We'll order the pizzas after everybody else gets to my house, so I think that's about everything we need."

Leah frowned. "You're forgetting one essential—dessert!"

"What's wrong with me?" Abby said, laughing. "What should we get? Cookies?"

"Brownies?" suggested Leah. The girls exchanged a glance.

"Both!" they said at the same time.

"Come on, desserts are in the next aisle," Leah said as she pushed the cart around the corner. Suddenly she backed up—right into Abby!

"Leah! What are you—," Abby began.

But Leah frantically waved her hands at her friend and whispered, "Shh! Shh!"

"What? What is it?" Abby asked as she followed Leah to the opposite end of the aisle.

Leah leaned close to Abby's ear and whispered, "Max! Max Menendez! He's right over there getting candy! Do I look okay?"

Abby reached out and smoothed out the bumps in her friend's blond ponytail. It was no secret that Leah had a major crush on Max. Every time she was around him, she got so nervous that she could barely speak. "You look great," Abby assured Leah. "Want to go say hi?"

"Are you crazy?" Leah gasped as she tried to get a

glimpse of her reflection in the freezer case's shiny silver handle.

"Come on!" Abby urged her friend as she gave Leah a little push. "This is a perfect opportunity to talk to him! I'll come with you."

But Leah shook her head. "I'll probably say something stupid," she replied. "Let's just wait here until he leaves."

"Come on, Leah!" Abby whispered. "How will you two ever go out if you won't talk to him? And this'll be a great story to tell Chloe and Nora at the party tonight."

"Party? What party?" a voice asked.

Leah and Abby spun around.

It was Max!

He smiled at the girls. "You're having a party and you didn't invite me?"

Abby looked at Leah, thinking it would be the perfect time for her friend to say *something* to Max. But Leah just stood there—as frozen as the peas across the aisle. Her eyes were so wide that she even looked a little scared.

"Um . . . of course we didn't invite you," Abby said, grinning playfully as she tried to save the situation. "It's a sleepover party. No boys allowed."

"Well, *fine*," Max said, pretending to be hurt. "I'm busy, anyway."

"Oh yeah?" asked Abby. "Doing what?"

"Wouldn't you like to know?" Max said with a laugh. "Nah, I'm just messing with you guys. I'm going to a movie with Jake and Toby. I thought I'd snag some candy before the show."

"That's cool," Abby said as her eyes lit up. She didn't notice the way Leah began to watch her. "What are you guys gonna see?"

"Don't know yet," Max replied. He laughed. "I mean, obviously some snacks were the priority, you know?"

"Well, have fun," Abby said. "We've gotta go. See you later, Max."

"See you guys," Max said. "Hey, Leah—heads up!"

Leah jumped as Max tossed a candy bar to her. "I got too much," he said with a smile. "You want one?"

"Uh, yeah, sure," Leah stammered. "Th-thanks, Max."

Max flashed another grin at the girls as he sauntered down the aisle. As soon as he was gone, Leah grabbed Abby's arm. "Wow! He *gave* me *a candy bar!*"

Abby smiled at Leah's excitement. "Kind of," she pointed out. "You still have to pay for it."

But Leah was too distracted to pay attention to Abby. "Max is so cute!" she gushed. "I wish I didn't get so tongue-tied around him."

"Just relax," Abby said to her friend. "He's only a boy."

"Only a boy!" exclaimed Leah. "How are you not as in love with him as I am?"

Abby thought for a moment about Max's spiky black hair and his big smile. He was definitely a hottie—but there was a guy at school who Abby thought was even hotter. "Yeah, he's pretty awesome," she said carefully.

But Leah gave Abby a piercing look. "You think there's somebody cuter than Max?" she asked. "Who?"

Abby pressed her lips together and shook her head. Her crush was top secret—and she wanted to keep it that way.

"Oh, come on, Abby," Leah begged. "I told you a million years ago that I liked Max. You owe me!"

Abby laughed. "I'm not telling. It's not my fault you can't keep your own secrets."

"I'll figure out who it is," Leah said. "It's not Toby, is it?"

"Not even close," Abby replied. "Now would you please stop? I'm not telling!"

Leah clapped her hands. "I know! I know! It's Jake, isn't it?"

Abby's mouth dropped open. "No! Why would you even think that?"

"*Jake?*" squealed Leah. "Seriously? You like *Jake?*"

"No way," Abby said firmly. "Please, can you drop it? I mean it, Leah."

Leah sighed. "Fine, be that way. But I *will* find out for sure who you like."

Abby was silent as she pushed the cart toward the produce aisle to get some strawberries for breakfast. She knew that when Leah was determined to find something out, there was no stopping her.

And Abby also knew that even though Leah was her very best friend, she couldn't keep a secret. Leah might be shy around boys, but she wasn't shy when it came to gossip. Abby knew she meant well, but telling Leah something in confidence was as good as posting it online.

Before long, the whole world would know it too.

WANT MORE CREEPINESS?
Then you're in luck, because P. J. Night has
some more scares for you and your friends!

THROUGH THE LABYRINTH

Uh-oh! Looks like you're stuck in the twisted
labyrinth of the Metaxas Sculpture Garden! Can
you find your way out before it's too late?

YOU'RE INVITED TO ...
CREATE YOUR OWN SCARY STORY!

Do you want to turn your sleepover into a creepover? Telling a spooky story is a great way to set the mood. P. J. Night has written a few sentences to get you started. Fill in the rest of the story and have fun scaring your friends.

You can also collaborate with your friends on this story by taking turns. Have everyone at your sleepover sit in a circle. Pick one person to start. She will add a sentence or two to the story, cover what she wrote with a piece of paper leaving only the last word or phrase visible, and then pass the story to the next girl. Once everyone has taken a turn, read the scary story you created together aloud!

I love volunteering at the library after school. Sometimes I read to little kids or help the librarians plan activities, but the one thing I hate is going down into the basement. The library is ancient, and the basement is dusty and moldy and crumbling. Spiders spin webs in between the rusty old bookshelves where we store the books that are too damaged to be checked out.

Today started out like any other volunteer day, that is, until the head librarian asked me to help sort books in the basement for the library's used-book sale. As I walked down the steps, I saw that a dim light was already glowing in one corner.

"Hello" came a voice from the darkness. . . .

_____

_____

_____

_____

_____

_____

_____

_____

_____

_____

_____

A lifelong night owl, **P. J. NIGHT** often works furiously into the wee hours of the morning, writing down spooky tales and dreaming up new stories of the supernatural and otherworldly. Although P. J.'s whereabouts are unknown at this time, we suspect the author lives in a drafty, old mansion where the floorboards creak when no one is there and the flickering candlelight creates shadows that creep along the walls. We truly wish we could tell you more, but we've been sworn to keep P. J.'s identity a secret . . . and it's a secret we will take to our graves!

THE HIDDEN WORLD OF
Changers

In this electrifying new fantasy series, four normal seventh graders find out that they are Changers, a line of mythological shapeshifters that history has forgotten.

But there's little time for questions. A powerful warlock is racing toward their town, destroying everything in his wake. Can Mack, Gabriella, Darren, and Fiona harness their newfound powers in time to save their home?

Find out in The Hidden World of Changers series!